+ya

FIC
Brook

**Port Carling
Public Library**

Brooks, Bruce.
　Boot / Bruce Brooks. --1st ed. --New York :
HarperCollins, c1998.
　122 p. --(Wolfbay Wings ; #4)

"A Laura Geringer book."
Boot, an orphan, dislikes some of the more physical
aspects of hockey, but in protecting his younger sister
from a bully, he learns that aggression can be
appropriate at times.

(SEE NEXT CARD)

359　　　98JAN27　　　　　3733/pc　1-502999

# BOOT

## Other Novels by Bruce Brooks

Asylum for Nightface

What Hearts

Everywhere

No Kidding

Midnight Hour Encores

The Moves Make the Man

## THE WOLFBAY WINGS

Woodsie

Zip

Cody

Prince

# BRUCE BROOKS

A LAURA GERINGER BOOK
*An Imprint of* HarperCollins*Publishers*

## For Fred

Harper Trophy® is a registered trademark of
HarperCollins Publishers Inc.

Boot

Copyright © 1998 by Bruce Brooks

Library of Congress Cataloging-in-Publication Data
Brooks, Bruce.
    Boot / by Bruce Brooks.
        p.      cm. — (The Wolfbay Wings ; #4)
    "A Laura Geringer book."
    Summary: Boot, an orphan, dislikes some of the more
physical aspects of hockey, but in protecting his younger sister
from a bully, he learns that aggression can be appropriate
at times.
    ISBN 0-06-440680-6 (pbk.) — ISBN 0-06-027569-3 (lib. bdg.).
    [1. Hockey—Fiction.   2. Bullies—Fiction.   3. Brothers and
sisters—Fiction.   4. Orphans—Fiction.]   I. Title.   II. Series:
Brooks, Bruce.   Wolfbay Wings ; #4
PZ7.B7913Bo     1998                                     97-39674
[Fic]—dc21                                                   CIP
                                                              AC

Typography by Steve Scott
1   2   3   4   5   6   7   8   9   10
❖
First Edition

Visit us on the World Wide Web!
http://www.harperchildrens.com

# BOOT

# one

The Columbia left wing who is supposed to be checking the Boot glances over his shoulder as he skates into the neutral zone to chase Prince carrying the puck. Sure enough, as the wing thought, the slow old Boot is trudging along, head down, a few steps behind, losing ice with each stride. Looks like he *might* make it to the blue line after the play has been completed and they have to turn around to come the other way, and then he'll have to stop, turn, and do it all over . . . .

The Columbia left wing decides he can cheat a little on his coverage—he doesn't like the way that little kid Cody is trailing Prince into the zone with some stop-and-go moves that are giving fits to his teammate, the Columbia center. Sure enough, as the wing watches, Cody turns the center the wrong way and slips around him clean to the other side, now trailing Prince without any check.

In half a second the left wing decides to abandon his slow-Boot responsibility back there; he darts to catch up with Cody and slash at his stick from behind. Cody veers hard left as Prince speeds up on his way down the high slot, stickhandling, hypnotizing the defenseman skating backwards in front of him, drawing the dude's eyes down at the puck, where the left wing knows he shouldn't be looking.

Prince skeets almost to a stop and circles tightly to make what he obviously thought would be an easy flip pass to Cody cutting in behind the D from the left circle. But the dutiful Columbia wing who left old Boot in his ice chips has kept after Codes and now manages just to hook his right glove enough to spin him a tiny bit upright and sideways as he cuts to the net. Cody wobbles slightly, but it ought to be enough to make him miss that pass, which is no doubt zipping right now to intersect his unimpeded dash at the net. *Yes!* thinks the Columbia wing, *I broke up the play!*

The only thing is, Prince, although he is looking right at Cody, does something else entirely. And he seems to have been planning on it all along: He snaps a low blind backhand pass the *other* way, past the defenseman to the *right*. Is he nuts? There can't be anybody over *there* to get the puck! It will go to the corner and the Columbia D will pick it up and skate it out of the zone. The left wing, still hooking Cody's glove, looks up—as does Cody, now coasting nice and slow—to watch this happen.

But instead of Nobody over on that side, instead of harmless blank ice, there is Someone, someone planted at the far post with his skates spread and his stick drawn back eight inches, ready to one-time that pass into a gaping net. It is, glory be, the old Boot. Just as the Columbia wing is thinking "How did *he* get here?" Boot's stick—only the stick, none of the rest of that cloddish body—moves in a blur through those eight inches and the next thing you know, the puck is bulging the old twine behind the sprawling goalie like a cannonball.

The Columbia wing lets his stick blade droop to the ice. Cody and Prince are rubbing the scorer's helmet as he turns, without even raising his arms, and trudges back to his bench. "Hey, nice freakin' coverage," the Columbia goalie screams at his wing.

"Your little sister could check that dude." The wing ignores him, staring at the far post, where the Boot was waiting for that perfect blind backhand pass from Prince. But—how?—the guy was way back there and—

Well, it's a sad common tale. But the fact is, the Boot leaves a lot of broken hearts on the ice . . . .

The Boot's Lesson One in Goal Scoring: Disappear. Lesson Two: Show up at the last possible moment, just as the puck arrives. Lesson Three: Do the simple thing and put it in the rope.

The hardest part is learning how to disappear. Maybe it's even one of those things you can't learn; maybe it's just a gift. If so, the Boot has always been blessed with it. The Boot was born to disappear.

ost of the nuns who taught at the orphanage where the Boot grew up were not exactly what people think nuns are supposed to be. It is true they seemed like they didn't mind being quiet and doing boring stuff as much as people from outside minded, but the nuns would tell you that's just because they always had God to think about, so they were never *completely* bored. But none of them were especially *committed* to boredom or anything, committed to having no personality or interest in all kinds of junk that outsiders imagine they would never think about when they could be kneeling and closing their eyes or, in the classroom, standing erect and scowling and swatting students with rulers when they gave wrong answers.

Well, it wasn't like that. The Boot got swatted only once in about seven years, and that was not because he gave a wrong answer, but because he put

Superglue on the seat of a certain jerk's desk in Latin class and refused to admit he had done it even when the teacher found the tube in his jacket. Otherwise, the nuns were pretty cool as far as teachers go.

One of them, Sister Jean, who taught science, had a saying that the Boot liked and has always remembered. Sister Jean wanted students to spend most of their class time trying to answer very tough questions she asked, questions that went just far enough beyond the chemical formula for salt or the different types of clouds or whatever. The students didn't usually want to do that much thinking and didn't want to risk saying something dumb. So Sister Jean, who was also the basketball coach, came up with a slogan to make us dare to get foolish.

"The only shot you cannot make," she often said, "is the one you do not take."

Later maybe I will come back to this and tell how it made me think about what kind of hockey player I was, when I got around to hockey my first year out.

The orphanage. The orphanage. I could say it all day and it would never sound like the place I lived, ate, went to church, went to school, and watched other kids hustle their way into families. If somebody in my life now hears the word *orphanage* they get all big-eyed and tender and look at me like I started life with only one leg or something. I have no idea why. What does the word *orphanage* mean to people who have never lived in one? I have read a few Charles Dickens novels and stuff like that and I guess people, especially adults, get this idea *orphanage* means a nasty dark damp place where poor pitiful orphan children are fed cold oatmeal three times a day and whupped a lot. Maybe some are like that, but most are not. Anyway, if you grow up in a place, no matter what it's called that place is what you think of when people say home.

No one has ever told me what happened to the original Mr. and Mrs. Boot except they started skating on that great rink in the sky when I was not old enough to notice they had left. I don't mean to sound disrespectful, and of course their name was not Boot, which is just a nickname I got later, but the fact is, I *don't* remember them. I have never been all that curious about them either, though every now and then some goody-goody adult encourages me to share my sincere deep feelings of desperate longing and mystery, usually by joining some dorky group of orphans who sit around and try to say things that make them sound like they give a fat deal about a past they can never really recall and certainly cannot go back and change so that everybody stays alive and together like the TV shows you see on reruns in black and white.

The thing I remember most about life in the orphanage is the coming and going. It was hard to make friends or even enemies, because some guy you liked or hated might only be there three weeks and then one day you never saw him again. I learned there were basically two kinds of kid there: guys who put most of their skills into being highly visible (the majority), and guys who tried to play it cooler and hang back and be invisible (only a few).

Visible is what you wanted to be if you hoped to get picked fast by one of the families that came to check us out. Every Sunday a bunch of these people drove up; they were usually waiting in chapel for us to file in and sing hymns in choir and do all the duties around the altar and sit looking smart and thoughtful and just happy enough during the incredibly long, dull sermon. Some guys were just plain geniuses at getting strangers to pick them out; I knew quite a few kids who never had to go past their first Sunday before someone took them home. (Some of them came back later. We called them "re-jects.") It was pretty bad to get returned, though the rejects always pretended to be *relieved* to escape from the horrible homes they had been taken to.

The Boot kind of seemed to stick around longer than just about anybody, with the kids who were deaf or had a twisted arm or were incredibly ugly or something like that. After kindergarten started, which I guess was some kind of indication about a kid's prospects for getting adopted, the nuns started to treat me like I ought to be feeling pretty awful, but I didn't. I wasn't deaf or ugly, but I was very tall and bony, and I had noticed the cute little guys were the first to go every Sunday. One nun read me this really obvious book about a big ol' dog in the city pound that nobody would adopt because they all chose cute li'l puppies, or were afraid he would eat too much or hurt their sweet kiddies, or something. Eventually, as you might guess, a cool guy takes the big dog just *because* he's big and old and smart, and—surprise!—it all works out splendidly forever after. The cool guy even lives on a ranch or something where the big dog can run his heart out. Hooray!

Actually, it was a pretty cool guy who eventually chose the big, old Boot, too. He didn't look all that cool at the time, certainly not like the dude in the book, who I remember was always wearing sharp windbreaker jackets with the collar snapped up and his hair combed. The man who took the Boot was much older, heavier, and balder than the book dude. He was alone, too, which was not how people usually came to choose a kid; they were required by law or something to come in couples, but the nuns seemed to know this guy and didn't make an issue of how he was alone.

After he asked to meet me and we were introduced and shook hands, before he even spoke to me he shoved a photo at me and waited while I looked. It was a black-and-white picture of a lady in a bathing suit holding a large striped beach ball with the ocean behind her. She was smiling at the camera and looked pretty nice, but the picture was also pretty old.

"That's *Mrs.* Baxter," the man said, taking it back and looking at it quickly as if he wanted just to make sure. Then he put it in a pocket and shook my hand again and said, "I'm the *Mr.* Baxter who goes along with her."

Mr. Baxter had very pink skin and no wrinkles at all, though the hair around his ears was starting to turn from some dark color to white. He wore a black double-breasted suit that had *plenty* of wrinkles, but I don't remember caring much. I had never seen a double-breasted suit before and I thought it looked extremely cool. I had a slight idea that suits like that didn't exactly go along with high-top white sneakers, which is what Mr. Baxter was wearing, but what the heck.

Soon enough I found out why he wore the sneaks. We hadn't stood there outside chapel for more than a couple of minutes when he suddenly smacked himself in the forehead and said, "But of course—you're very concerned about my age!"

"I am?" I said.

"Sure," he said, starting to trot out toward the

playing field that was way over near the place the cars were always parked on Sundays. "Absolutely nothing wrong with that. You ask yourself, 'Can an old fellow like this do the job? Can he take care of the father-in-situ business, the fundamentals, the playing-catch and wrasslin'?' It's okay, really—such doubts are natural."

By this time we had jogged out to the very center of the farthest field. I suddenly noticed there was a dirty soccer ball sitting on the ground there, black and white octagons and lots of dried mud. Mr. Baxter looked tremendously surprised to see the ball—I think he was goofing—and strolled up to it and, still talking about how I must be legitimately afraid of being locked into some home with a "male adult authority figure" who sat in a legs-up lounger in front of the TV all evening and went to sleep with a crumpled newspaper and a half-drunk can of beer on his stomach (actually, this *is* what Mr. Baxter did most nights, minus the beer can, and it was a book instead of a paper), all the while he was kind of rolling the ball back and forth with the toe of his left sneaker. And then, without breaking his speech or grunting with the effort or anything, he toe-popped the ball straight up, hit it a couple of times with his forehead, then let it fall, and just before it would have hit the ground a few feet in front of him he launched his heavy body forward with this incredible grace and swung his left leg in an arc that seemed nine feet long. There was this *pop* sound and I could barely follow the ball as it flew straight as a laser beam into the top right corner of the soccer goal sixty yards away.

I looked back at him. My mouth was probably open. He looked kind of ashamed, but he was smiling a little too. "That's it for the showing off," he said. "Now, wanna kick it around a little?"

The Boot had never played soccer; the nuns were your basic sport types and that is all we were allowed to organize at recess. But in half an hour Mr. Baxter taught me how to dribble, make a couple of elementary fakes with the ball, pass along the ground with either foot, and strike shots with both feet too. He was as good as Sister Jean was at teaching, maybe better. I always liked learning stuff, and he kept two steps ahead of me just right, and before you knew it I was all wrapped up in learning soccer from him. Then he stopped, looked at his watch, and said, "Well? Shall we go home? Mrs. Baxter is making meat loaf."

My impulse was to ask if we could just keep playing, but I knew this was it, so I nodded. He kicked the ball toward the parking lot, and it rolled and stopped six inches from the bumper of a very old green Buick. We went and got into that car. I almost asked him what would have happened if the ball had stopped in front of the orphanage's 1957 black Chevy pickup parked two spaces away. Would we have taken *that* car, then? But I didn't. Just climbed into the Buick, noticed that the seat slanted pretty bad to the right and had a seatbelt made out of an old leather belt stitched with thick thread onto the back of the seat. I fastened it kind of around my chest area, and off we went.

We had driven in silence for maybe ten minutes when Mr. Baxter did his smack-forehead-jeez-I-forgot number again and reached over to my side and fisted the dashboard above the glove compartment, the door of which—I noticed there was no handle on it, just a hole—dropped open. Watching the road more or less, he stuck his hand in, scuffled it around, and brought out another photo, which he held out until I took it.

"The family," he said. "Names and ethnic affiliations on the back."

It was like one of the UNICEF posters we were always having to put up in the orphanage. There were an unbelievable number of kids, from babies to probably age seventeen, in an unbelievable number of skin colors and hair types and clothing styles. Some of them smiled for the camera, some of them scowled for the camera. Silently I counted them, and just as I reached my sum Mr. Baxter spoke it.

"Eleven," Mr. Baxter said. "You're the twelfth, and the final complement. I've always thought 'twelfth' was a very fine word. Have you ever noticed—"

"There are *eleven* other kids?"

He nodded enthusiastically. "Eleven very *interesting* kids."

I grunted, crossed my arms, and refused the obvious invitation to ask him to elaborate. This was a surprise. It is true that I had been extremely diligent during all those years in the orphanage at refusing to speculate about what it might be like to get adopted. But of course I studied the thing from a slight distance when it happened around me, and also I couldn't help speculating a *little*. Most of the kids who got adopted were adopted as only children. That is how my fantasies went, too: I was always the only kid, with two adults. I worried about being unable to escape the constant attention an only kid must get all the time, but I also enjoyed the idea of being numero uno, too.

Never had I looked at the possibility of being numero twelve.

In the car, still without speaking, I flipped the card over. As Mr. Baxter had said, the names of the kids and words like *Burmese-American* and *Sioux-American* and so on were written on the spaces where the backs of the heads would be. Some of the names were goofy, some were just normal names. I flipped the photo back into the glove compartment.

"Interesting," I said, so as not to look like a complete spoiled and disappointed jerk. "I look forward to meeting, um, *all* of them."

"Yes," said Mr. Baxter. Then, after a pause, as if he knew just what I was thinking, he said, "You may actually find it more comfortable to slip into a large family after years at an orphanage than you would if it were a very small one. There's a lot of space in this group, and not much pressure. But we *are* a *family*. That *will* be different."

"We'll see, I guess," I said. He nodded. I felt like something else was called for. So finally I looked over at him and said, "Thanks. I mean, you know, for—"

"You're welcome," he said, smiling. "Literally. You are welcome."

So the Boot thought about what it meant to be welcome, all the way home.

# *three*

*H*alfway through practice Coach Cooper blows his whistle at center ice and waits while we all skate over and slide onto our knees around him.

He looks us over. "Shark, get a new chinstrap," he says. "And Cody, I don't want to tell you again to wear your mouthguard even during drills."

He clears his throat. "Okay. We are exactly half-way through the season. Does anyone know what that means this year?

Zip, our goalie, raises his hand, looking serious and good-boy, and after he gets a nod says, "It means we get to suck for *exactly* as long as we already have, sir."

Coach ignores him, as do all the other players. Finally Woodsie, without raising his hand, quietly says what we all know.

"Checking."

"That's right," says Coach Cooper. "Up until

our next game, we have officially been playing a non-contact sport." There are a few laughs. "We have not been officially entitled to hit people. We have not had to worry officially about being hit *by* people. I trust you all know that by 'hit' I mean something that has nothing to do with fists or temper. It has to do with skating at an opponent, usually the puck carrier, and, without lifting your arms or your elbows, skating right *through* him and putting him down hard on his butt. Or it means slinging your hip into the guy trying to speed up the boards past you and either pinning him there like a dead bug in a science project or, once again, knocking him onto his butt."

Dooby raises his hand and says, "I can't help noticing that the butt seems to be a large factor in the matter of hitting or checking—"

"And of course it means the other side too," Coach goes on, blowing Dooby off. "It means that when *you* are cruising up the boards with the puck, you might *plan* on zipping past the defender sliding over towards you sideways, only to find all of a sudden that he has jacked you into the glass with a well-timed punch of the hips, and *you* are on *your* butt, hurting, and the puck is gone and so has your stick and you don't have any idea for a second where you are. *Or* . . . it means you, Woodsie, or you, Dooby, skate back to pick up the puck after their forward dumps it into the zone, and you are skating along behind the net nice and easy as usual on your forehand and you just glance down to make sure you've got the puck flat and just then, as you come around the post with your head down, out of nowhere somebody clocks you and you fly backwards into the boards and by the time you straighten your helmet so you can see, the puck has been put into the net in front of you."

"Now just a *minute*," says Zip.

"It's a different game with hitting," the coach goes on. "It's real hockey. It's the way it will be from now on, as long as you play, through high school, college, whatever. Some games there won't be five good hits the whole game among both teams. Some games you'll feel like there was nothing *but* hitting—you won't remember even touching the puck, and you'll be black and blue in places you thought those three-hundred-dollar pads protected you."

"Not black and *blue*," says Dooby. "I look just *awful* in black and blue. Maybe if I upped it to five-hundred-dollar pads—"

"We've tried a few drills this year," Coach says, "but you didn't take them seriously, just used them as an excuse to whack each other around, so I decided not to waste the time until you had gotten a little experience. Until you *wanted* to learn how to take a check, and how to get a guy back for it."

"In other words," Cody sighs, "until we've *suffered*." He looks up toward the ceiling and raises his palms. "Why, oh why, does it always need to come to suffering? Can't we all be brothers who—"

"It's the biggest adjustment you will ever have to make in this sport," Coach finishes. He looks around at us. "Some of you will love it, and be smart with it, and—surprise!—all of a sudden you'll be much more effective players. Some of you will hate it, or fear it, and hide from it, and—surprise!—you will find you don't count nearly as much as you used to. He shrugs. "We'll start seeing on Saturday."

"My brother broke his wrist last week checking somebody," Cody says brightly. "Out for the season. Cries at night, too. He's sixteen. It may even heal crooked, and already two of the colleges—"

Coach Cooper, who happened to be Cody's dad, cuts him off, annoyed. "That was a very poor hit," he says, reddening a little. "Your brother went in late, and high, and tried to forearm a bigger kid back into the nineteenth century. If you hit like that, you're asking for it. *We* won't hit like that."

"And if we do break a wrist, well, hey, we got *another*," says Dooby helpfully.

Despite the joking there is a general air of seriousness and thoughtfulness in the circle of players. You can see them thinking, not about breaking a bone, but about which kind they'll be—a hitter or a hider. I raise my hand.

"Boot."

"Some people avoid the whole matter, do they not?" I ask.

"You mean, some people—you, for instance— have until now managed to sort of sneak around— skillfully, Boot, skillfully—and slip beneath everyone's notice now and then? And might such people be able to keep doing so, without getting *hit* any more than they got *seen* before? And might they be able to avoid hitting anyone either?"

"Any more than they had to bother to cover someone *defensively* before?" Prince adds in Coach's voice, and almost everybody laughs. They mock the Boot because he chooses to spend his energy putting the puck in the net instead of lifting people's sticks in the neutral zone and such stuff.

Coach Cooper studies me for a moment while the others laugh. Then, a little more quietly than he was speaking before, he says, "I'd advise you not to count on it, Boot."

Now everybody has switched his eyes over to look at me. I don't acknowledge either their attention or the coach's warning.

"And I'd advise you of that," he says, "not only for the sake of your goals." He makes a quick show of glancing around the circle at the guys watching me, and comes back to my eyes. He raises his eyebrows. "Know what I mean?"

"No," I say. "Not at all."

"You will," he says. "The first time we are flat and cold as a team, and somebody delivers a great hit to cause a turnover, and—well, you'll feel it."

Then we scrimmage. Nobody hits anybody. I get two goals. Then, right at the end, as Prince is coming fast across the red line, he looks down because the puck has dragged and he wants to pull it up to speed, and as he looks down, Woodsie, who has been backskating to cover Prince's rush, suddenly darts forward and crashes into Prince and sends him flying. He lands hard. The puck skittles away unnoticed. Everybody has frozen. They watch Woodsie, standing there, arms down, stick blade on the ice, and Prince, who has pulled himself up from flat on his back to his elbows as he stares at Woodsie. It is silent. Not even Coach Cooper says a word. Down at the end of the rink we hear the Zamboni driver, quieter than usual, open the board gate.

Finally Prince says, "Man, you *killed* me, Woodsie."

"Sorry," says Woodsie and his shoulders start to droop.

"Don't be," Prince snaps. "Just make sure you do it four or five times to guys wearing brown jerseys on Saturday, okay?"

"Okay," says Woodsie.

"Okay, then," says Prince, starting to get up. "That was awesome. I can't wait for it to happen to people we hate." The Zamboni starts. Prince skates over to Woodsie with his hand out. When Woodsie sticks his out to tap it, Prince grabs him by the elbow, slips a skate behind Woodsie's heels, and with a yank and a twist dumps him flat. Then Prince turns to the rest of us, holds up both arms cocked like he was showing big muscles, and says, "I survived . . . the Hit!"

Almost everybody laughs. Almost all of the tension goes away. Almost.

nd how was *your* game today?" Baxter gets around to asking me, as he passes the creamed corn, almost all of which is gone from the huge serving bowl.

I scrape most of what is left onto my plate. "I didn't have a game," I say. "I just had a scrimmage."

I don't usually call attention to my scrimmages during the Dinner Hour Review of Achievements of the Day, as one of my sisters calls it when Baxter and Mary make a point of giving each kid who had something important happen that day a chance to tell about it. For one thing, I don't like to talk about my stuff. For another, I play way more "real games"—games that count officially in the league my team belongs to—than any of the others who play basketball or wrestle or do gymnastics or play in the chess club or act in plays, so I would get to talk more than them anyway, without going down to the scrimmage level for my material. It seems kind of piggish. Last, a couple of my brothers seem to hate hockey and don't think all that much of me, either, and they use every chance they can to show their scorn and superiority.

Anthony jumps on the scrimmage thing. "Ooh, a real live *scrimmage*," he says, raising his eyebrows as he butters another piece of bread. "Hockey scrimmages are *so* thrilling."

"Yeah," says Jojo, who worships Anthony and wants to be him, though Anthony is black and tall and graceful and plays basketball as if he were born to do it, while Jojo is squatty and white and muscled sideways instead of up-and-down, which means he should probably spend his winters wrestling. But he plays hoops, since Anthony does. He stinks, too. He just took up fifteen minutes telling us about a "practice game" in which he finally scored in double figures (11). He looks at me with a kind of snarly grin.

"How'd the scrimmage go?" Baxter persists.

"Fine."

"Did you obliterate your teammates?" asks Anthony.

"Not especially," I say.

"Did you score?" Jojo asks.

"Couple goals," I say. "Two." I hold up fingers. Jojo's eyes narrow in hatred.

As if he is psychic, Anthony, who has finally finished buttering his piece of bread and now holds it in front of his eyes, studying it critically instead of looking at me, says, "And did you beat anybody up?"

Anthony (and of course Jojo) tried for weeks after I arrived from the orphanage to welcome me into the family by beating my ass in a two-on-one fight. They insulted me, mocked me, poked me, bumped me, even directly challenged me in boxing pose, but I wouldn't fight them. I hate fighting. Eventually Anthony and Jojo had to resort to beating me up in my bed in the middle of the night, and since then Anthony, I think, has hated himself for such chickenpoop behavior, as much as he has hated me for "making" him do it.

"Nope," I say, looking at him. "Didn't beat anybody up, not two-on-one with a helper, not even all by myself."

Anthony flicks me a nasty look. Baxter, who I think has a good idea of what's beneath all this, says, "Yes, well, of course Boot is in a league that disallows fighting, in fact imposes a mandatory two-game suspension, if I recall—"

"Not talking 'bout *fighting* necessarily," Anthony says coolly. "Isn't there such a thing in hockey as . . . *hitting?*" He takes a bite of his bread at last. Beside him, Jojo snorts and mutters, "Hitting! In hockey!" (They both play football in the fall.)

"We've been penalized for checking, until now." I find myself saying stuff and wishing I wasn't. Anthony sneers, but I go on. "But after the halfway point of the season we are now allowed to check. To hit."

"Fighting?" says Mary, sounding alarmed as she starts the biscuits on another circuit. Only three are left in the basket. I hope one makes it this far, but it is doubtful.

Anthony and Jojo snort in unison but I ignore them. "No," I answer her, "not fighting. But where you used to have to kind of avoid crashing into people to knock them off the puck or out of their moves, or where you used to be forbidden to spook somebody by banging him against the boards every time he skated into your part of the ice, you can now do so." Mary nods, frowning, not quite getting it, or maybe getting it all too well.

"You can now do so," mimics Anthony.

"Right," I say. Why am I blushing?

"Or, quite without your permission, others may do so to *you.*"

"Sure," I say. "chance you take. This isn't bowling or jai alai. It's *hockey.*"

Anthony smiles, looks over at me, takes in my blush. "Well," he says, with a broad smile, "maybe this hockey thing just got a little interesting."

"Two goals is really *good,*" one of my smaller sisters finally chimes in, a little late.

"Thanks," I say. "It was just a scrimmage."

"And it was just *hockey,*" Jojo says, thinking he's being witty. He looks to Anthony for approval, but Anthony ignores him.

"Might have to catch one of those hard-hitting games," Anthony says, smiling. "Love to see some bodies fly, you know?"

"Absolutely," Baxter says. "I think—Mary, is it next weekend or—?"

"I'll check the calendar," Mary says. She and Baxter make a point of attending at least one official contest/presentation for each kid each season, which means they have an orderly but crammed calendar written out as soon as we all have our schedules at the start of our seasons. In general, their two lives are so hectic I don't know how they keep up even with stuff that's a lot more crucial than soccer games. (Sometimes they don't keep up.) Anyone from the family can come with them to watch anyone else, but very few of us ever catch a glimpse of each other in action.

Why am I worried that Anthony just might make good on his threat—that's what it is, coming from him—to attend one of my games? All I do is score a bunch of goals, at least one every game; nothing there to be ashamed of, right?

Sure. For the moment, we'll ignore the prospect of those flying bodies. I reach for the biscuit basket. It's empty.

# five

As we dress for our game there is obviously something different in the air. The jokes are halfhearted. No one throws tape balls. Looking around in sneak peeks, I catch almost everybody frowning at one time or another. Only Barry and Woodsie seem to be as cheerful as usual, but since these two are among the quietest guys on the team, the most serious, their smiles of anticipation really stand out. Finally I ask Barry why he is so chipper.

He tightens a skate. "Because at last instead of letting these zippy little skinny skater-guys slip around me, finally I get to throw a hip in their way and watch 'em *sprawl.*"

I look at Woodsie, who is grinning inside his helmet. He wears a red mouthguard, and his grin is an ugly thing. He catches my eye and nods in agreement.

Dooby, who has frowned a little, but less than

others, chimes in. "That's straight. Man, we've been having to watch these dipsy-doodle types that call themselves 'breakaway artists' and 'snipers' and such crap, we've been having to *watch* them and *let* them scoot around or stand in, hoping that, Please, Sir?, nice and polite, we could somehow do a bit of defensive playmaking."

"Offense, offense, offense," Barry says, with a nasty laugh. "Until now, that's who's gotten all the breaks. The pretty scorer types." He smacks his stick hard against the cement floor. Several players jump. "Well, wake up, pretty scorers! You're about to taste a little D."

"And it tastes a lot like ice in your face," says Dooby.

I wait a few seconds, and Woodsie says it: "But we shouldn't be rude, guys. Boot's a scorer. And we need his goals."

"Yeah, but he's not a *pretty* one," says Barry, as if this were a special lack that commanded respect.

"The Boot finds a higher number on the scoreboard to be very pretty all in itself," says the Boot.

The three of them laugh. "But you're not a

dipsy-doodle, wussie-type scorer," Dooby clarifies. "You're a hacker out there. You'll be all right. Nobody's gonna take *you* off your game by hitting you a few times."

"No way," Barry agrees. "You're tough, Boot." Woodsie says nothing.

Coach Cooper comes in for his pregame talk. He mentions a couple of guys to watch, says their goalie is weak on low shots, especially glove side, and adds that one of their star defensemen can be suckered into rushing the puck all the way up ice but will turn it over easy and give us an odd-man rush back the other way, because he's too lazy to skate catch-up after his big offensive play.

"Oh, and the checking," he says, as if it were just a minor afterthought. He looks around. "Anybody afraid of getting hit hard?"

Woodsie, who always knows his moment, raises his hand without hesitation. After a minute a few others join him, including Prince.

"Fine," Coach says. "Most of the rest of you are probably liars. There's nothing wrong with being scared of taking your first big hit, or even your second. But after that, you'd better notice that you aren't hurt, remember you're a hockey player, and get into the spirit of things. If you're too uncomfortable and want to wait until we've bashed each other around at Monday's practice, speak to me and I'll go light on your shifts. And it goes without saying, we don't stop playing hockey in order to start playing Hit the Bad Guy. Otherwise . . ."

We take the ice. We warm up. The horn sounds. As usual, my line starts: me, Prince, and Cody, with Woodsie and Dooby on D. The Boot has to admit he is nervous. The Boot is *never* nervous. The Chevy Chase winger the Boot will cover looks over and says, "You're gonna lose some teeth, jerko."

The Boot does not dignify this with a reply. But when the puck drops, the wing lunges straight at the Boot and hits him in the face mask with both elbows. The Boot falls backwards and smacks his helmet pretty hard on the ice. In fact, for a minute he doesn't know entirely where he is, though he manages to wave off the faces crowding around him. He is yanked to his skates. Looking around for the winger, he doesn't find him. He does see his own mouthpiece about twelve feet away.

"Try the box," Woodsie says from behind. The Boot looks. Sure enough, the winger who hit the Boot is sitting in the penalty box. On the scoreboard, two consecutive two-minute minor penalties are registered. The ref is saying something to the benches about keeping things under control. Then he drops the puck. Four minutes of power play. The Boot should get at least one.

But three times the Boot fans on centering passes that scuttle beneath his stick, and twice he starts to go for a loose puck around the goal only to find himself spinning on his butt a moment later, with a dull pain in the kidneys.

With thirty seconds to go in the second power play, Prince, panting from the long shift, says, "Come on, man. Stop jerking your head up at the last second."

"The Boot does not jerk his head up," I say.

"Yeah? Then how come the Boot has scuffed some very sweet centering passes that usually get buried? Don't let that jerk's hit get to you, man. And when those guys in the slot cross-check you, whack 'em without looking and then concentrate on the puck."

The Boot tries to follow whatever part of this advice may apply. But he misses another pass—yes, he notices, he *did* jerk his head up as the puck came close—and the Chevy Chase center picks it up in the corner and starts roaring up the boards on the Boot's side of the ice.

Angling toward him, the Boot hears a huge rumble of anticipatory noise from the Wolfbay bench, and celebratory whoops of violent satisfaction from Dooby and Cody nearby on the ice. The center looks up and meets the Boot's eye as they approach each other, and the Boot sees what he finally realizes is fear in the kid's eyes, as if he were begging the Boot "Don't kill me, please!" But then the kid sees something in the Boot's eyes too, and in a flash the center's fear is replaced by cheerful meanness.

His path and the Boot's converge along the boards at the blue line. The Boot hesitates—yes, he does—and then slides his hip sideways, not as hard as perhaps he could have. His hip just glances the butt of the center, who is already past the Boot with the puck, and the Boot hits the boards, loses his skates, and falls. Before he can get up, he hears whoops of derisive joy from the Chevy Chase bench.

Apparently, a shorthanded goal has been scored. The center took it all the way down.

"Nice check, feeb," says Prince, pulling the Boot to his feet. "Now you've used up your alotted amount of fear, okay? Get ready for the next one, and *hit* the sucker. It's not hard. If you can shoot pool, you can figure the angles, all right?"

But it doesn't work out that way. Without exactly being able to say why, the Boot misses several other checks, while finding that his usual strategy of vanishing seems to leave him untouched and open only when he is far out of scoring position. It is a mystery. The Coach yells a few things but the Boot doesn't catch them. Woodsie whispers a few tips but they mean nothing to the Boot. Then, seeming a little sudden, the final horn blows and the Boot looks up to see that we have lost by three goals. The Boot did not score.

In the locker room the Boot is quiet, as he usually is. But no one says anything to the Boot, or about the Boot, which is not quite normal.

The Boot, shouldering his bag, starts to look

forward to Monday's practice. Then, for the first time ever, he realizes that actually he does *not* look forward to Monday's practice. In fact, for the first time, he dreads it.

## six

**W**hen I joined the Baxter family four years ago, it didn't take me long to figure out each kid. I was used to scoping out people in groups and how they fell into this or that kind of link with others, this or that kind of habit. I was used to figuring out stuff like whether there was a big difference between the way the kid actually lived and the way he wanted the people around him to believe he lived. It's just a matter of keeping your eyes open and noticing things. Patterns. Most people find their way into some kind of pattern. You can work the whole thing out once you get hold of a piece and follow along.

Naturally I knew my own style of living, my own habits, my own patterns. And of course I put them into play in this new home just as I had at the orphanage, just as I later did on the ice. It's simple, really. It's what I've already said about my-self: The Boot likes to cruise in the spaces where no one looks, to disappear, to avoid the scuffles, but then to pop up when opportunity calls.

Once Anthony had beat me up, he lost interest in tailing me, and it was easy to slip away into the margins of life in the house. I was surprised to find that there was already someone in the family who lived pretty much the same way I did. Even traveled the same paths and hung out in the same places around the house and yard: I kept finding evidence, fresh apple cores or footprints or a sweater left behind. It was a girl, and she was a little older than me. Once I knew that, I decided it must be the one who called herself Kit, because she fit the stats and she was rarely to be seen. It wasn't long before the inevitable happened that confirmed she was the one. We found ourselves arriving one day at the same gable in the attic with a book and a cushion, to read by the sun that came in that window until about noon.

At first I was kind of pissed off. Kit was playing my game. She was in my space. But Kit is pretty cool. She didn't make a big deal of the coincidence then, and she never has. We don't talk about what we are doing, slipping by on the edge of life, being loners mostly, spying on everybody else. It's like, "Okay, obviously we are alike, so what?" After a while we got to talking about things a little, though, and if I had to choose I would say she was probably my best friend among all my sisters and brothers.

A few weeks ago after dinner I made one of my usual stops, a low-slung apple tree way in the back of the totally messy backyard that was something between a jungle and a junkyard. The Boot hit this place maybe every other night, when the house got him cockeyed with noise from everybody making deals with everybody else to do each other's homework and the ice cream we had for dessert every night kicking in with its sugar crazies and the littler kids getting cranky and tired while the older ones got cranky and bored. The Boot liked to get a little air at such times.

As the Boot climbed the first few branches of the apple tree, he saw a couple of whitish, hazy, small shapes out of the corner of his eye, above and to the left, out in the thinner branches where the Boot could not go because he was too large, and he knew they were Kit's bare feet dangling. He didn't say anything and neither did she. He spun and sat on a branch in the middle of the tree, near the trunk, and for twenty minutes he just watched the house. Only two things happened during that time—Jeremy, supposedly a health-freak Ethiopian, snuck out of a third floor window and stood on the gutter so he could quickly inhale a cigarette, and a boy and girl whose faces you couldn't see ran on tiptoes out the door from the screened porch to kiss a few times in the shadows, and then ran back in. Not much of a show, but then the Boot did not come here for a show.

After a while Kit said, "I finally got the curve in."

"Cool," said the Boot. "Nobody else has it."

"Yeah. It makes the game slower, but the players have better moves. More realistic fakes and angling and stuff. All the others have the guy just cut two impossible ninety-degree turns to get around some- body." She snorted a laugh.

Kit has a deep secret: She is writing the software for a new computer ice hockey game, which she is convinced she will "market" to a big game com- pany. She is one of two or three other kids who were adopted when they were past being babies.

She won't talk about where she came from, but she has always had the idea of inventing something that would make her a lot of money. I think it's because she thinks money means freedom one day, and she was probably poor. She might have even lived on the street. After March 1 she won't wear shoes except to school, or a coat either, and she never seems to get cold. She bathes only when forced to. I have never seen her smile. She is not especially hard or skittish or anything; she is smart and even kind, but just always serious.

Apparently she is also a computer genius or something. She really has written most of this hockey thing, and she wants to make it more like real hockey than the other ones on the market. That's how she thinks her game will "differentiate" itself from them, while—she hopes—still selling at a similar pace (she picked a hockey game to invent because for some reason hockey computer games sell better than any other kind except the famous combat ones). She has come to a lot of my practices and sat off by herself taking notes. She has noticed lots of things I never thought about, one of which is that skaters don't really move in straight lines if you look at them from above, as the computer games all do. Skaters curve to the left, and then curve back to the right, then to the left again, and right, and so on. Kit says if you drew a straight line on the ice and told a skater to follow it, he would never skate *along* it, but would just keep *crossing* it back and forth as he flew along "straight." In other computer games, the skaters move in straight lines.

Tonight, after a while she says, "Tell me about hitting."

The Boot's muscles all kind of contract and he almost falls off his branch. "What do you mean? What have you been—"

She cuts the Boot off. "It's not like in the other games, where two players just smack into each other and both of them stop dead and fall down on the spot. I know it isn't, not in any of the games I've watched on the Deuce. There's a lot more glancing-blow kind of thing, where players sort of collide but slip off each other and keep going, but slowed down and in new directions. What about it? What does it *feel* like?"

"Why do you always ask what something '*feels* like'?" the Boot replies, sounding maybe a little cranky. Maybe more than a little.

Kit says nothing. The Boot figures she is reacting to the way he answered. He has always answered her questions before in a good-natured way, always willing to help, bringing up specific points she didn't know to ask about. She has offered three times to cut him in on the deal, ten percent, to show how grateful she is for the help, but the Boot has always said she should keep all her money, he's just a hockey player and it's no big deal for him to talk about what he knows. But now . . . Well, the Boot is sure she knows something's funny about the way he snapped. After all, it was the Boot himself who told her she had to get her software to reflect what hockey *felt* like . . .

"And anyway," the Boot hears himself go on, "why do you want to include 'hitting' in your game at all? I mean, it's not like it's an official *skill* or anything, like skating or stickhandling or poke-checking or shooting. It's like a half-skill or some-thing, like nothing more than a sort of *gesture* sometimes, and sometimes a kind of cheat, a crude way of messing *up* a play without *making* a play. I mean, why bother?"

Very quietly Kit says, "It's a part of hockey."

"So is fighting," the Boot says louder than he wants. "But you won't have *that* in your pure precious game, will you? That was a big, like, principle with you, wasn't it—'No fighting on *my* ice,' you said. So—"

"Hitting is different," she says, and the Boot can hear the sigh she tries to keep out of her voice. "Look, just forget it for now, okay? Forget I brought it up."

"It's not like recklessly crashing into somebody is—"

"We'll do it whenever you're ready," she finishes.

"I'm ready to tell you right now," the Boot says, putting his hands on the limb and pushing himself off to the one beneath, and on down, until he jumps to the ground, a little too far too fast. He feels a pop in both knees, but they're fine.

"I'll tell you," he says, looking up, seeing the hazy spot that is her white-blond head and pale face, "what it *feels* like. It feels like a car wreck. Like walking on a sidewalk downtown feeling safe and suddenly getting hit from behind by a bicycle messenger jerk in a big hurry. It feels like you can't expect it but you can't think about anything else. It feels *awful*. It *sucks*. Okay?"

From way above, she says, "I'm sorry." Then she adds, "You'll get used to it. You're a really great hockey player, you know."

The Boot makes a disgusted noise and strides off across the yard, shaking his head. He's not at all sure *what* he knows.

t the first few practices, everybody is trying to do nothing but show how macho he is, how brave, how *physical*. Players leave their skates to launch themselves like slow rockets anybody can see coming, and people *do* see, and get out of the way most of the time, and the pitifully airborne checkers slam into the boards all alone or crash to the good old hard-as-stone ice. I figure they can't keep it up *too* long before they notice they are a bunch of fools.

The Boot, however, remembers he's there to play a little hockey, and for most of the time he does so. In fact, he gets away with murder, skating deliberately around all these distracted check-nutty bodies and getting the puck and dropping the goalies with a shoulder fake before a snap shot, bingo.

The Boot's escape is not complete, however. Twice the Boot gets clocked, once when he has just received a bouncing pass and is teeing it up, but suddenly ends up cracking his shoulder blades against the ice and losing his stick and his bearings at the same time, not to mention the puck, not to mention the big G(oal).

"Good hit, Woodsie," says the coach from somewhere, and the Boot supposes it was. The Boot *was* about to bury it, and a defenseman stopped him. Fair enough. The Boot does not like it, but, okay, under a certain broad definition you could still call it hockey.

The second hit is from Cody, who is lined up on D tonight so we can get the feel of playing against a small speedy defender like the coach's son on the team we play next. This one, this hit, does not strike the Boot as fair at all. The Boot is cruising nice and subtle just behind the main line of action, out of sight of anyone who didn't know to look for him, ready to pounce, zip in for a quick mystery score, zip away. But Cody knows the Boot's game, and takes advantage of that to wait until the Boot is practically standing still, watching the puck in the corner, waiting to see if his guy comes out with it, in which case he will just kind of slide along the outside of this circle and set up at—

*Pow.* Cody, way out of position, comes in hard and low and his shoulder catches the Boot on the back of the thigh and the Boot does a complete flip and ends up on his hands and knees, and a second later he pukes through his face mask onto the ice. There is a great deal of laughter.

"Can't stand around anymore, Bootster," says Cody as he skates by.

The Boot, finished with his puking, says, "You only knew to hit me here because you're usually on my *line*, you jerk."

"Oh, otherwise you're, like, invisible or something?"

"Yes," the Boot says.

But Cody is shaking his head. And Dooby is suddenly there too, looking down, and he says, "How long do you think you can feed off these teams and go unnoticed, Boot? Couple of goals a game gets you kind of a little attention, a little look-see, know what we mean?"

"The Boot can deal with that. There are places to skate—"

"Not if you're on your butt," says Cody.

"Yeah, well if—"

"That's the great thing about a good put-down hit, Boot. It's kind of a preventive thing, see? Takes you out of the play in advance."

"Yeah," says Cody, "and you know that if *Dooby* can figure that out all by himself, other defensemen are already *way* ahead of him. They've got your number on their dartboards, Boot."

"You're gonna get popped," Dooby adds.

"Constantly."

"And once those guys see how you—"

Coach Cooper skates up. "Okay, stop gloating, Cody; get out of here, Doobs. Boot, you all right?" He chucks the Boot a water bottle and the Boot squirts his face mask clean, rinses his mouth, then sprays the upchuck on the ice up against the dasher so no one will have to skate through it.

"Thanks," says the Boot, handing the bottle back and getting to his skates. Coach hands him his stick.

"Listen, Boot." Coach is Frowning with Concern.

"Yes?"

"Can I . . . do anything for you? Do you need, you know, some—"

"Yes," I say. I wave my hand at the team on the ice. "You can tell these *children* to stop playing tackle football and start letting the Boot get on with his hockey."

"Well, Boot—"

"And if you say 'Well, Boot, hitting is a *part* of hockey!' again I will puke through my face mask for the duration of the scrimmage." The Boot spits neatly through an aperture in the mesh. "Hockey is *pretty*. It's not just crashing."

Coach nods and looks away, stretching his neck and scratching it lightly with the curled fingers of one of his ancient smelly old brown leather gloves. After a minute, still not looking at me, he says, "Did you happen to notice Cody's left cheekbone tonight?"

"As a matter of fact I did. It seems to be blue in color."

Coach nods some more. "Brother hit him with a steel spoon. Stainless steel. Back of the spoon, that nice hard curve, *smap*."

"*Jerry* did that?" I gawp. "But Jerry is the biggest goody-goody saintly boy that ever—"

"I still kind of like him too," he says in a dry

tone. "But yes, my older son Jerry does tend to be a little angelic. But." He shrugs, and looks at me with a little smile. "Family life, which is supposed to be at least as pretty as hockey, can get a little rough sometimes. Cody's cheekbone is cracked, actually. Just a little." He looks at me closer. "You know what I'm talking about, right? You must fight with *your* brothers. Jeez, you got enough of them. I bet—"

"The subject was hockey."

"Excuse me," Coach says. He straightens up and looks a little more formal. "I'm sorry to say it, Bootster. I've been waiting through almost three weeks of practices and games. Unless you start learning to mix it up a little in the tough parts of the ice, I'm going to have to drop you a line. Maybe two."

The Boot sputters. "But I have led this team in goals five seasons running, except for Moseby, and I free Prince and Cody to run around and be creative and count on—"

"That's what I mean," says Coach. "Can they count on you anymore? And I don't mean just to be at the side of the net at the right moment."

"What else *do* you mean? What else *matters* if the Boot is there?"

"Ignoring for the moment that the Boot is *not* there these days, let's talk about what else I mean." He leans close. I smell the years of sweat rising off the gloves he rests his chin on, clasped over the top of his stick. "The fact is, Boot, when a team starts hitting it starts kind of keeping track of a few new things."

"Such as?"

He sighs. "Such as, who has guts? Who will do the dirty work for his teammates? His *share* of the dirty work? Who is brave? Loyal? Who watches out for his smaller teammates to see they don't get bullied out of their game? Who is willing to turn a flat team into an excited team by taking a big painful hit for them all as they sit there on their lazy butts? Stuff like that."

"You're saying . . . you're saying, or my 'Nice Goal!' teammates are saying, that the Boot is not 'loyal.'"

He shakes his head. The Boot goes on.

"You're saying the Boot is not 'brave.'"

"That's not—"

"Nor especially hardworking or inspiring, certainly not 'tough.' That's what you're saying. And because of this, the Boot is being closed out."

"Look," Coach says, "this is still just the first couple of weeks—"

"But the signs are clear, aren't they? You can tell, and they can tell, these *teammates* of mine. You can all tell the Boot is not attracted to the 'physical' part of the game, right? And thus everything else the Boot does is severely discounted in value."

"Stop."

"No. I won't. You started this. Drop me a couple of lines? Because I get dumped by my own right wing who sneaks up on me? And who evidently now dislikes me behind my back, with all the rest of them, dislikes the cowardly, awkward Boot who used to be okay when he was carrying the team with his goals."

"Carrying *what* team?" says Prince, who was skating by but skeets to a stop. "You can only carry a team that sets you up with the puck, man." Coach tells him to get lost and Prince skates away with a glare at the Boot.

Coach says nothing for a few minutes. Neither does the Boot. He has said all he is going to say, and in fact considers skating off the ice and calling this scrimmage quits a half-hour early. But just as the Boot is about to push off, Coach speaks.

"I'm a hockey coach, Boot, and hockey is a simple game. All I can do is offer to teach you some things if you want to learn, so you can continue to be the team's best right wing. But if you don't adjust—well, then, you'll probably *stop* being the best right wing. And your place on the top line—not to mention your place in the respect of your team—may suffer."

"Well," says the Boot, pushing off the boards and backskating for a few feet so he faces the coach, "well, then everything ought to be *really* simple and easy, shouldn't it?" The Boot swivels and skates frontwards for a few strides. Then he stops and looks back at the coach, who is still watching him.

"Nice and simple," says the Boot. "Know what? I envy you that." Then the Boot turns and skates to the boards, bangs on the glass for the gate to be opened, and heads off to the empty locker room. Behind him he hears a moment of silence, then the noise picks up again.

## eight

t the orphanage there were always a couple of guys who apparently got a thrill out of fighting, and I saw a lot of the scuffles they started. It was always a surprise. I'd be walking somewhere or standing and talking to someone or just sitting by myself, when I'd hear some wild-animal noises nearby—grunts and whines, mostly—and I would turn and there they would be, two people thrashing around, swinging their arms wildly, falling, crying, whatever. It did not take a genius to notice that a few particular kids were always involved, with some one-timer as an opponent. It seemed like there were always three or four of these jerks; as soon as one would get adopted or sent away, another would come. They never fought each other.

The fighters were not what you would call nice kids. They were generally as mean as wasps, and they had no conscience. You'd watch one walking down the hall ahead of you talking to someone, and you'd see farther ahead a kid with his back to the hall traffic, head bent over the combination lock on his locker or something, and you'd watch as the fighter walked by this guy and, without breaking his stride or varying his concentration on what he was yapping about, sometimes without even looking, usually without bothering to stop, the fighter would snap an elbow into the locker-kid's back, right between the shoulder blades, and keep walking, leaving the kid with his face smashed against the steel locker or crumpled and moaning with his hands scrabbling behind his back, trying to reach the place that hurt. Stuff like that. These were jerks, these kids. Not quite human.

Their fights never seemed to amount to much. They would swing and poke, the other kid would swing and poke, all the blows would seem to glance or miss, and before long the fight would be nothing but two red-faced boys grappling each other, panting, with their eyes full of hate and fatigue. It was pretty much the same whenever I watched a pro hockey game on TV and saw a fight there. Lots of motion, no damage. Big deal. Still, there *did* seem to be a lot of tension . . . .

I hated the fighter-kids, hated their meanness. The trouble was, I was also fascinated with them in a way—or maybe it's better to say I was fascinated with whatever it was they got out of fighting. I watched and watched, but I couldn't figure this out. Where was the fun? The self-respect? Little by little I got closer and closer, my curiosity pulling me in, until finally, one day, without planning to do it, I started a fight myself.

It wasn't with a fighter-kid, of course. It was with a kid named Raymond, a small kid who yanked on the little loop on the back of my shirt until it pulled off, yelling "Fruit loop! Fruit loop!" People did this all the time and never got more than a snarl or a curse over the shoulder in retaliation. But when Raymond grabbed my loop and started to yelp, I pivoted on the ball of my left foot, raising my fists as I turned, and then hit him once with each fist, bang bang, square in the face. It was the worst thing I have ever felt.

To my amazement, Raymond collapsed like a popped paper bag, spurting blood out of his nose and mouth, spitting teeth, wailing, coughing, gagging—I thought I had killed him. I stood there gawking.

A nun ran up and pushed me down the hall, saying something about how it would be okay because she had seen him "assault" me first and so on. I had never been in a speck of trouble, while Raymond was always doing little annoying mischief things. But in fact I knew it would not be all right at all. Look what I could do! I was a monster.

I saw Raymond once more, two days later (he spent the time in the infirmary), from the window of math class, as he walked out the front door of the dorm with a suitcase and got into the truck and was driven away somewhere. I could see both of his eyes were black, and his nose was huge, which meant I had broken it, and his lips were twice their normal size. Another kid told me there had been three teeth lying on the hall floor; he had grabbed them, Would I like to see? I said I would not, and a minute later I went to the bathroom and threw up.

When Anthony and Jojo beat me up in bed as a welcome to the Baxter household I hoped they would break my nose, but they didn't. Nor did they knock any teeth out. In fact, they mostly punched me in the chest and neck and stomach and back. This hurt plenty, maybe even worse than the face would have, but it left only bruises no one would see unless I walked around naked. Smart. The only bruises that might have shown were on the undersides of my forearms, because as they jumped me I came out of sleep and threw my arms in front of my face by instinct, before lowering them a minute later.

Tonight, at dinner, despite the fact that she keeps her hands in her lap as much as possible, I see the same kind of bruises on Kit's arms.

I look around the table during dinner, but I never see her look at anyone, or see anyone look at her. So after the meal I follow her quietly as she makes one of our usual escapes, and find her with a book in a dormer in the attic where we have sneaked a big candlestick and a bunch of candles. She has the new X-Men comic but she is not reading.

"Don't," she says to me, hugging herself and hiding her arms.

"Who did it?"

"I fell down."

"Sure. You're *so* clumsy. I've seen you climb trees, remember? Who did it? Why?"

Why? That much she *will* answer; I can see she thinks it might satisfy me and let her wriggle free. "Homework," she says.

"One of the boys wanted you to do his homework and you refused and he beat you? That's what happened?"

She says, "Who says it was a boy, anyway?"

I reach out and pull one of her wrists free. She doesn't resist. I study the bruises. I can see now that there are a couple of layers. Some are older. She's been beaten a few times.

I lay her arm down along her leg. "Okay," I say, "what subject? At least tell me that."

She thinks. Then she shakes her head: it will give her tormentor away.

She's right. I know which guys are weak in which subjects and it would take me no time to figure out who it was. But I have already figured it has to be Anthony or Jojo. And I can't see Anthony doing something as wussy as this. Anthony has his pride, at least a little. But only one person is so lowdown he could hit his younger, peaceful sister.

"It was math," I say. "And it was Jojo."

She blinks for a second, then sighs. "Computer science actually. Some crappy graphics anyone could have done."

"But it was him, wasn't it? It was Jojo."

She doesn't bother to answer. Now, she looks at her own left arm with mild curiosity, holding it up to the candlelight and studying the bruises. Finally she lowers it, and looks at me.

I try to speak with anger, authority. "Why didn't . . . I mean, you and I are like *friends*. Why—"

"We *are* friends," she says with a kind of sad resignation. "That's the reason, in fact. He would kick your butt, even though he's really kind of a weenie."

I am almost sputtering in outrage. But I notice I am still sitting there, speaking in a whisper. "How can you say that? How could he kick my butt, just because he does"—I gesture at her arms—"*this* to girls? And anyway, so what?"

She yawns, looks at me sleepily. "Okay," she says. "It's like this. You're honorable. You're my friend. You've got a bigtime sense of right and wrong. So, naturally, you'd stick your big strong chin into his face and poke your finger in his chest and announce that you were going to kill him for the cowardly thing he did."

"So?"

"So then he'd laugh at you and beat the crap out of you. Because even though you are smarter than he is, and just as big, and a better athlete, he could look in your eyes and see that you don't really want to fight."

"What do you mean? Look at me. I'm . . . I'm—"

"Yes," she says, giving me a calm glance, "sure, you look furious. I'm sure you *are* furious. And I appreciate it, Boot, really I do." She reaches out an arm and pats my hand on the attic floor.

I swallow, and wait for a minute. "Are you saying I'm—"

"No," she says, picking up her comic book. "No, I am not saying you are a coward or anything like that. I happen to know you are very brave, in fact. But"—she opens the comic and looks down at it, probably so she doesn't have to look at me—"you are just not a snake-hearted jerk. And that's what you have to be to fight a snake-hearted jerk like Jojo."

I shrug and try to think of something to add. But I can't, so I leave her alone. On a second-floor landing my eight-year-old sister from Laos is trying to throw my seven-year-old brother from the coal mines of West Virginia over the railing. I break them up and send them off for cookies in the kitchen. And I think a lot about what Kit said. I try to make myself feel noble for not wanting to hit people, for not being "snake-hearted" and all that. It doesn't work. After all, you can't just sit back and let the snake-hearts take over everything because you're so *nice.* There must be something you can be, something decent, that makes you feel just fine punching out Jojo—or blindsiding a left wing at 20 mph. If so, why didn't I have it? Woodsie and Cody and Dooby and Ernie and Shinny all had it. They weren't snake-hearted.

Was I a coward? Was I afraid to hit, and to get hit?

I go to my room and take out some paper and make a list. On one side I write TTFAGH (Things to Fear About Getting Hit). Each thing underneath gets a number grade showing how serious it is, with 1 being low and 5 high. Here's what I write:

# TTFAGH

**Pain: 2**

**Injury: 4** *(Who wants to wear a cast or have your jaw wired shut?)*

**Reputation with adults: 2** *(I figure they know I'm not bad or mean.)*

**Reputation with kids: 1** *(If anything, being known as bad in hockey would be a* benefit, *not a drawback.)*

I think for a while. There's something missing from my list, something that bothers me, more than a 1 or a 2, even more than a 4, something that isn't as easy to explain as this obvious stuff. I close the book and get out my history homework and am halfway through an essay on Rosa Parks when it hits me, and I yank the paper back and write on it:

**Distraction: 5**

That's it. I sit there and stare at the word, letting Rosa Parks fade. Getting hit or making a hit in hockey, or throwing a punch in real life, means that you drop what you were doing and concentrate on the Hit. The Hit becomes all there is. You can't do everything at once: Either you're going to cruise and sneak and set up for the quick pass to fire into the net, or you're going to look around to get ready for a hit that might be coming, nothing else. Either you're going to live your life and do your homework and eat your meals, or you're going to lie in wait, all pulled tight like an arrow on a bowstring, so you're ready to pop the guy you want to pop.

It is so hard to play hockey. You have to do all kinds of tricky things, while all the time ice-skating through various sets of obstacles. To become good at ice hockey takes several different skills mixed just right so they work together, plus good skating, plus a strategy, one that fits with the previous two—your skills and your skating.

Is it any wonder that once you get it all going, you want to be able to concentrate and *keep* it going? Instead of having to keep one eyeball spinning around to see the perimeter in case some crude fool is coming to crash into you and wipe out forty seconds of very subtle work? Instead of having to chuck your strategy all of a sudden so *you* can crash into somebody—and not just to "make a play" but also just to demonstrate to your loyal teammates that you are willing to punish your body "for the team"? Well, maybe any team that requires a stupid hit instead of a couple of crisp goals on the scoreboard is not the team for me.

I spend the rest of the evening trying to see how this hooks up with protecting my sister from a bully in the house. I get nowhere with that one.

**A**t the orphanage, the Boot found he was pretty happy staying cool and watching other guys get all worked up, trying to figure out what would make them appeal to people who would take them home. They chose certain ways to wear their ties or to roll their lapels or to show their cuffs, ways to comb their hair; they decided whether or not it would look good to be in the choir, to show they had to shave by leaving a little shadow or did *not* have to by scraping their cheeks and chins until they were pink. I kind of slipped away when they started checking each other out and worrying about who had a better chance. Maybe this had something to do with why I took so long to be picked. I guess I just was not the kind who liked competition.

Once, a person named Sister Mercy, who taught sports, spent most of a semester trying to get me to play harder during the parts of games she called "crunch time." I tried to do what she suggested, but I could never keep it up. I could not "read the situation" as she always said an athlete should; that meant I did not have a sense of the whole "story" of that particular game in my mind as it rushed toward its climax. It seemed like all I could "read" was the opportunities that opened up for me to do what I was good at, and just by doing it—spiking the ball at the net in volleyball, running down deep corner shots in tennis doubles and returning them with lobs, things like that—I was making a contribution to the team that satisfied me. At least that's how I saw it, and how I was comfortable.

But I got nothing but grades of C⁻ in physical education that year.

hree more games, three hundred more hits!!!!, three more losses.

In the first game, I did not even get a shot on goal, spending most of my time in the offensive zone on my hands and knees with my butt toward the cage. Once I seemed to be completely open to one-time the puck and it came and I snapped at it and, I swear, I felt the first edge of my stick hit the very outside edge of it, but then somebody ran over me and I was like a squirrel on a dirt road. Cody told me the puck ended up in the seats.

I got so desperate to make up for all this that I started wandering around the neutral and defensive zones just looking for somebody to smash. This was awful for two reasons. First, wandering like that—Coach calls it "headhunting"—takes you out of position and leaves your man uncovered; second, people on ice skates aren't all that easy to smash (except for me, I guess). By the time I lunged full-stretch at a defenseman in the third period and watched him scoot coolly away, I knew before I hit the ice in a humiliating belly flop that I was on my way down.

Sure enough, I missed every other shift that day, and for the next two games I was dropped to the third line, with Billy and Shark. Billy and Shark! Shinny, who took my place with Prince and Cody and who was still playing with a cast on his broken wrist except he'd shaved it down with a wood plane until it fit inside his glove, scored a goal each game and somehow managed to crunch every opposing player who strayed within ten feet of him. I watched, but I couldn't figure it out.

"Shinny is not a mean person," I said to Barry on the bench, as we watched the little guy in glasses and a shaved cast clothesline a huge winger who had thought he might rush the puck past the dweeb. The ref had to call time out to help the kid off the ice. Shinny pretended not to notice. Every person on his shift managed to skate by and swat him in the shin guards with a stick blade, same as saying "Way to play!" I was incredibly jealous.

"No," said Barry, thinking hard, "you're right. He's not." A couple of seconds later he added, "I guess he's just good at *acting* like he is."

I snorted. "Acting," I scoffed.

Barry cocked an eyebrow at me. "So?"

I kept watching the ice. "So, if I wanted to do 'acting' I'd join the Drama Club and put on those cheesy plays every spring. Personally, I'm here to play good, straightforward hockey."

Barry was looking at the ice again. "Seems to me you used to like to act—to act like you were invisible."

"That was a strategic optical illusion," I said. "It's completely different from putting on a fake snarl and whacking people in the helmet."

"Ah," said Barry. "I see. Well, whatever he's doing, Shinny's got me convinced. I don't even want to go near him in practice."

The rest of those games I watched Shinny, and Woodsie, and Dooby, and Cody, all of whom seemed to *love* knocking people off the puck or taking a knock while carrying the puck themselves and staying upright and in possession. As far as I could tell, none of those guys gave up much of his skill or speed in trade for the hitting. But when I tried . . .

One player I noticed tended to avoid hits was Prince. He had a cool little sidestep move when he would tuck the puck and let somebody trying to cream him whiz by and cream the boards instead. When he had the chance to nail the other team's puck carrier, he just used his lizard-quick poke check instead. At the end of a power play the line change got mixed up and I ended up on the ice with Prince. He got to a loose puck all alone, softly lofted it up the middle of the ice, and skated hard for the bench, head down. A huge defenseman from the other team watched him and took a path that intersected Prince's and he hit him, full-speed and head-on. Prince's body completely left the ice and his helmet even came off, before he hit flat in a back flop.

The goon who'd hit him just skated around Prince in little circles, grinning. I watched, but then I felt something funny. I looked up. Every single person on the bench, including Coach Cooper, was staring at me with this grim look of expectation.

It took me a minute, but then I got it: I was supposed to "avenge" Prince, by skating over and wiping out the goon. This made me mad for a minute, but then I think I actually decided to try it, and I might have, too, but by the time I had made up my mind the goon was on his way to his bench. Woodsie flew off our bench for his shift but went straight for the big guy and cross-checked him so hard under the chin that *his* helmet came off and he fell backward and snocked his skull on the ice. Woodsie got a screaming fit from the other coach (which he ignored) and a game misconduct from the referee (which he didn't) and a stick-thwacking-the-boards standing ovation from the Wings (which he pretended not to hear). But when I climbed in to sit, everybody just shut up and looked the other way.

After the game and the silent locker room, I was walking with my bag toward the bus stop when I heard Dooby call me. I glanced at him and couldn't think of anything to say. We just walked for a while. Finally he said, "You know, Zip is going to cut the laces in my skates before the next game for this."

"For what?" I said.

"Being seen with you. You're bad news."

"Am I *that* awful?" I said, a little startled.

He looked like he was thinking hard. "W-e-l-l-l-l, let's just say the only thing you could do to make yourself worse is if you managed to become one of those girls who think they can play hockey and ought to be allowed on the team and put on a good line and not have to play any messy physical defense or anything, all because they're a girl. *That* would probably be worse." He nodded. But then he added, "Maybe."

"What was so bad about me today? I mean, jeez, I tried to knock down that center in the first period—"

"Yes, but you see, he didn't even have the puck and as it was, you missed him and they turned it into a three-on-one and scored—"

"—and I kind of tangled up that defenseman behind the net in the second—"

"Yes, I recall, but you only touched him with your elbows, after dropping your stick too; the ref called you for 'bowing and they scored twenty seconds into the power play."

"—and . . . and . . . aw, man, who really cares. Just let me get on track and put a couple in the string and nobody will give a hoot whether or not I could hip-check the stinking Zamboni."

He didn't say anything. When I looked over, his forehead was wrinkled and he was frowning a little, like he was trying to remember something bad so he could tell me gently. But he didn't tell me gently after all.

"You see, Boot, the trouble is you're a complete wuss."

"What do you—"

"You should have done something, *anything*, to that big jerk who hit Prince today. You—"

I was spitty and flustered, waving my arm with the two hockey sticks in it. "But—but—you were there, you've been watching, you've seen how, how, how I, I just make an idiot of myself when I try to check somebody. It—I hate to admit it, okay?, but there's got to be, like, real *technique* to it, and I don't know how to take it or give it, I just *miss* and end up on the ice looking *stupid* and . . ." I trailed off, miserable.

Dooby waited a second, then said, "Looking stupid is better than looking like you don't care when some enemy beats up on your teammate."

"Well, sure, but—"

"And besides," he said, frowning thoughtfully, "you've got it wrong. You've got the whole thing wrong, about checking, hitting. You're waiting to learn some, like, some 'proper way' so you can 'execute' the Hit with your brain. But you don't hit from your brain, Boot. You hit from instinct, from your gut, from a sense of what's called for, what you just feel you *should* do, on the spot."

"Well," I said, "I *have* worked hard to develop my game in a way that—"

"Bunch of bull, Boot. I mean, come *on*. Can't you see? Do you really think you disappear out there? Do you think you're really so teeny and sneaky you can cause A-team players under A-team coaches to, like, 'misplace' you for even three seconds?"

"But then how—"

Dooby smiled at me and shook his head. "But then how do you score all of those goals, if it isn't by this goofy little oh-I'm-invisible thing you've dreamed up? How?" He stopped and jabbed me in the chest with his stick blades, and he grinned. "Easy to figure that one out, amigo. You're *good*. You're a good hockey player. You're one of those incredibly lucky prima-donna sons-of-poodles who have that special instinct for scoring goals. God knows I envy you—so does everybody on the team. We sit there and watch and suddenly you've got another goal, and we look at each other and say 'How the flop does he *do* it?' But"—he jabbed me again—"I will tell you one thing. We all know this: You work very hard. And the other team works very hard to stop you. So if you score, it's no sneaky accident. You couldn't sneak into a dark barn at night, Bootster. No—when you score, it's because you are playing from your gut and you are *good* from your gut. All that strategy stuff is just something you use to keep your nervous energy occupied."

I said nothing. Neither did Dooby. But he didn't seem the least uncomfortable—in fact, while we waited he started whistling "Smells Like Teen Spirit," way off-key.

The bus came, and we both got on. We rode in silence. I thought about what he'd told me, but it was too much to get around, it required too much taking-apart, I was afraid I would start spilling little gearwheels and tiny axles and bolts and sprockets all over the bus, the nervous machinery behind the idea of myself as Invisible Man, the Great Strategist. I didn't want to believe I wasn't able to think myself into life and then out of it. I didn't want to rely on my gut, because I had no idea what my gut might do or whether I could even control it. Which, I guess, is the whole purpose of the gut as opposed to the brain.

Dooby got up as his stop approached. I grabbed on to his bag. "Doobs."

He looked down at me like he had forgotten I was there. "Boots. Yeah?"

Somebody else pulled the cord for Dooby's stop. "Let me just get one thing clear, okay?"

"Okay, but I got to—"

"I know. But if I understand you, you're saying I already play from instinct, though I believed I was playing, like, from my head. And I have definitely proven that I can't check and hit while trying to work through that supreme—"

He was moving toward the back door, nodding but nervous about the stop. "Yeah, Boot, right. But, like, I have to get home for dinner and stuff, you know?"

"So," I said, as he backed off the last step and

held the rear doors open for another second to listen, "so what you seem to be saying is that, like, if I stop *trying* to hit and just start letting the hits *happen*, then—"

"Yeah yeah, Boot, you got it, that's it exactly. Now I got—" The door closed. I sat back down. I sat there thinking so deep that I missed my stop and had to get off three stops away and walk back carrying my hockey junk, plus I left both of my sticks on the bus and never got them back. But by the time I walked up the front steps of the bright, noisy house and heard Jojo's mocking laugh above the voices of everybody else for a second or two, by that time I was smiling and I have a feeling it probably would have looked like something in between relieved and sly. Yeah—definitely relieved, and definitely sly.

## eleven

**A**fter dinner that night, instead of cruising my usual paths, I leave through the back door and cut through the weedy wooded lot next door and hit the sidewalk, heading west. I'm doing some intense thinking, but even so a couple of times I think I hear a small noise off to my right and behind me—the click of a twig snapped, the shuffle of leaves. Finally, after one muddy sound as if a foot is being pulled out of a suck, I stop, turn toward the darkness that way, and say, "Okay, come on out."

Ten seconds later a white head and some white feet appear in the dusk at the edge of the scrub oak.

"Hi, Kit," I say.

"Where you going?" she says.

I turn and resume my walk. "West, I think. Maybe west-southwest."

I hear her scurry along the edge of the oak behind me. "You know what I mean," she says, finishing with a sharp curse as she steps on something that hurts.

"I guess I do," I say. I stop and look back at her. She's still hanging back under the trees, still uninvited. "Listen," I say. "Have you solved your hitting problem yet? Have you figured out the software for the famous bone-jarring body check?"

"No," she says. She pauses, then adds, "Have you?"

I laugh. "No. No, I haven't. And I am starting to suck because of it. So I am going tonight to watch a Midget-A game at the rink, to see if anything sinks in. Those guys have been hitting for five or six years and I figure they must be able to do it pretty natural. Probably I could pick up a few, like, insights."

I make a quick motion to show she can come with me if she wants to. After a minute she's walking beside me on the grass that runs along the sidewalk. After ten or fifteen minutes she says, "I was at the last game."

I grunt.

"You probably didn't see me."

I grunt again.

"That's because I was sitting with this family, a

mom and three kids all in a row, and I just took the seat next in line like I was the next sister. They were all blond and dressed in Gap Kids, three girls. None of them gave a toenail for hockey or probably for their brother who was one of the scrubs on the team you played. They just sat there looking like they wished they could be off somewhere trying out a new hairdo for Barbie, but their mother was *really* into the game, insane into it, screaming and bouncing up and down and shaking her fist. She screamed at the ref all the time and once she even gave him the finger. Every now and then she would look down the line of her daughters and encourage them to join the fun. Once she noticed me, but at that moment I raised my arms and hollered the name of one of the kids she had been yelling at, so she kind of decided I must be okay even if I did not genetically belong in her party. Know what I saw?"

We are getting close to the rink. It sits like a crashed flying saucer, black and round and edgy too, against the dull blue night sky. "What did you see?"

"It's more what I didn't see."

I wait, but she is obviously delaying what must

be her big revelation until I ask for it. So I stop and face her and sigh. "Okay. I'll fall for it. What did you *not* see at our last game, Kit? What, oh what, was missing?"

She grins. "You."

I roll my eyes and turn back toward the rink. She grabs my sleeve; it feels like it has caught lightly on a thorn.

"I mean it," she says. "Really. It's like somebody took your uniform and put it on, with your number 9 on it and everything. But he couldn't fool anybody who knew the team, knew you and how you play. That was some other guy out there, like."

"And let me guess—he seemed awkward, out of place, unfamiliar with the way things worked, unskilled, *totally* unskilled. Does that about cover it, or have I left something out of the cliché?"

She shakes her head. "None of those things are right. There was only one thing that stuck out, one very simple thing, couldn't miss it—and once you saw this thing, you didn't need to look at stuff like 'skills' and all that."

"Okay," I say patiently, stopping twenty feet from the door to the rink. "Okay, what was it that showed up so clear in this player?"

She looks in my eyes. "Fear," she says.

"What? If you think I am afraid of coming into hard—"

"Not fear of being clobbered," she says. "Not fear of pain, even."

"Then"—I try to sound superior and uninterested—"then what was this phony Boot afraid of?"

She watches me. I look away toward the doors. When I don't look back, she goes ahead. "Fear of just *doing* something, without *thinking* it first. Fear of not hesitating, not evaluating, not taking the time to decide. You know how I've always told you I look up to you because you're so careful. *That's* what I mean: fear of not being careful."

I try to make a little laugh. "That's an awful lot to be afraid of. I thought you said it was something simple."

She shivers. Besides being barefoot, as always, she has no sweater. "Well," she says, "it is simple. Or at least the solution is."

"What is that?"

She startles me by grabbing my chin and

pulling my face close to hers. "Are you going to listen to me?"

I try to laugh again. "Well, I—"

"This has to do with everything," she says. Without breaking eye contact, she holds up her left forearm so I can see how bruised it is. "It has to do with how I get beat and how you feel and how *you* get beat and how you feel. Can you listen to me?"

I let my phony laugh and grin fade and look her in the eye. I am a foot taller than she is but somehow she seems bigger than me right now. She must be on her tiptoes, pulling my face down. She's serious, in any case. She's major.

"I can listen," I finally say. Then I hold up a hand. She waits, and I go on. "I can listen, but you know what? I don't think I need to. I think I've got it, all by myself. I guess. Maybe."

Still holding my face, she smiles. Then she drops her hand but holds my eyes with hers. " 'I guess,' " she mocks. " 'Maybe'? What happened to all that Boot pride?"

"All right," I say, taking a step for the door. "The Boot knows all he needs to know and everybody else can shut up." I shake my head. "Don't even dare to worry about the Boot."

She nods, and turns and walks away on the grass. I watch her hair like a white shadow disappearing, then I go into the rink for two hours of seeing how 190-pound teenagers manage to knock each other all over the ice while still playing unbelievably fine hockey. Wolfbay Midget-A wins 5–4 in overtime.

# twelve

hey were waiting for me at the corner of my street. They were shadows, but they weren't trying to hide themselves; I could even identify them by their silhouetted shapes: Zip was short and quick and seemed as he darted around to have been cut out of some shiny black film with a razor, Barry never moved and could have been a black snowman, Cody's face was always turned upward as if he was trying to get a moonburn, Prince leaned against the streetlight post with his arms crossed high and his legs crossed low and I was certain he was the only one who watched me approach, all the way.

By the time they could hear my footsteps they all turned and waited for me. Nobody said anything. For a second, I thought about stopping a few feet away, making it clearly a case of *me* and *them*. But I didn't stop. I walked right up to Cody and tapped him on the top of the head.

"'lo, Codes."

"What say, Booty."

I nodded at the rest of them. "Guys." They all murmured something in return.

There was a pause and then Prince and I started talking at the same time. I overrode him, and said, "Look, I think I know why you're here and I think I can save you a lot of trouble."

"No!" said Cody, whipping off his cap and throwing it hard to the sidewalk in disgust. "I knew it! But forget it, Boot—I won't let you get away with this."

I noticed Prince was laughing, so I gave him a look. He started to talk but laughed again, and this time everybody but Cody busted into laughter too. Cody just glared at me and steamed.

Finally Prince said, "See, Cody had to do this paper—"

"It was a 'thesis,'" Cody corrected him snootily.

"Okay, a thesis, whatever—something he had to write out as a means of solving some—what was it, Codes?—some social problem that was, like, making friends not get—"

"It was a thesis designed to extract a solution

to an intractable social problem proving divisive among a peer group." Cody looked at Prince with disdain. "Man, you couldn't summarize a comic book."

"Comic books come in English," Prince said. "Social studies does not."

"So I am your social studies problem?" I said, to draw the attention back to what was going on.

"Right." Cody nodded. "The hockey team is the peer group and the divisive element is your cowardly antisocial behavior—"

"The Boot has *never* been a coward," I said, feeling my anger kick in a little. "The Boot has tried to go along with these distractions and cheap kicks, but—"

"But you sucked, and you stopped," said Barry, staring at his feet.

"Right," said Zip, poking me in the breastbone with his forefinger. "When you were lousy at it, you gave up. Same old Boot. Just do what comes easy, and let the rest slide to somebody else."

"Scoring goals is far from easy," I replied coldly.

"But you have to admit it's easier for you than hip-checking somebody in open ice is, or pinning a fast guy with the puck against the boards."

"So? We each have our specialty." I poked Zip in the forehead. "If you shot pucks better than you caught them, wouldn't you be out there taking shifts on a line instead of hiding in your cage?"

"Hiding? Listen, you jerk—"

"I *believe*," said Prince, in a very loud voice, and because he is a singer he can really get some knife into it, "I believe that Boot must by now know what we are here to tell him. In case he doesn't, Cody, in the interest of his social studies project, should give him a quick overview. But Boot seems to have some speech of his own. We should hear Boot after Cody speaks. Cody?"

"Thank you, Prince," Cody said, straightening up, clearing his throat, and fixing me with this phony half-smile look as if I were his English teacher or something. "Boot. It has come to our attention that you are a screwup. When you didn't stand up to that bozo today it was too much to take anymore and we want you to know we all really think you're starting to suck *bad*. We want to be your friends, man, but if you don't start throwing your weight around then we will be forced to cut you out and treat you like a stray dog and you'll probably get so discouraged you'll quit hockey forever. There. I'm done."

Cody gave me a stern look. "Oh, and yeah, by the way. Shinny broke his cast in the game and fractured his hand again. So . . . well, you figure it out."

Prince caught my eye. "I think we ought to hear from Boot. We're bringing some heavy charges here. Am I right, Boot, in assuming you feel the . . . the *gravity* of the situation?" He raised his eyebrows at me. I nodded. "Well then. What've you got to say for yourself, Bootster?"

I looked at them. They all watched me quietly— Zip glaring with his ice-turquoise eyes, Cody looking simply interested, Barry sneaking peeks to the side as he studied his Reeboks, Prince holding my gaze, cool and without judgment—yet. The night air under the streetlight got very thick. Prince was right—no matter how much Cody goofed, they were telling me something you shouldn't ever have to tell a kid, because first, he shouldn't let it happen and second, he should know it for himself and fix it before anyone had to call him out about it: You shouldn't have to tell a kid that's he's letting you down, letting down the *team*, bigtime.

I looked at them. These were the guys I started hockey with, when we all still played with toy guns and trucks and stuff. I had just come from the orphanage. I never told them so, but joining up with them gave me something to be part of. I was grateful to the Baxters, but I knew from the start that my adopted family was going to be more like a crowded classroom at school than a cozy group. Zip, Cody, Barry, Prince. And the others they represented, from Shinny with his busted wrist to Shark with his big words and Woodsie with his big jump from being a kid all the way to being about forty on the ice. Here they were, and they were telling the Boot that the Boot sucked. Worse, that he sucked and he was a wuss about it. A coward. A selfish coward, protecting himself, looking for flashy goals, trying to skip the hard work.

Well, they were forgetting something: The Boot had pride. The Boot did not get to be the Boot by slacking and skipping. The Boot let no man say such things. Standing there in the spotlight, with bad words pointing at him in the air, the Boot had to conquer, he had to dig deep and come up with words of his own that would send these boys back home to bed with satisfaction. Yes. So, standing there, feeling the light on his face, the Boot drew himself tall and scowled, scowled at Zip, scowled at Cody, scowled at Prince and Barry. They looked afraid, all of a sudden. They looked respectful. They looked ready to listen.

"The Boot has one thing to say," I announced, locking eyes with each in turn. Then, my voice sharp and dangerous as a snap wrist shot, I said, "The Boot has let you down. The Boot has no excuse. But today is the first day of the rest of the Boot's life. . . ."

# thirteen

I was walking in the dark toward the staircase to the third floor where my room was, when I thought I might just check in on Kit. I don't know why. I'd never done it before. But I turned down the long hall toward the back of the house. As I walked I saw there was a light inside her room, showing out in a stripe beneath her door.

Then the door opened, and as he stepped out glancing back over his shoulder with a smug expression on his face I saw Jojo, with a couple of pieces of paper in his hand. He pulled the door closed and took three steps studying his papers in the dark when he came face to face with me.

For a second he looked scared, then confused, but then pretty fast he put on his usual cocky-bully sneer.

"You're smiling, hockey-boy. What's up?

Looking forward to a good-night kiss from your weirdo sister?"

I realized I was still wearing some shadow of the grin left from the long laughter that had followed my pronouncement out under the streetlight. I wiped it off now. "What are you doing here?" I said to Jojo.

He waved his papers in my face, flapping them just hard enough to touch my cheeks and nose and eyes. "Homework, hockey-boy. Good boys got to get their homework done, don't they?"

I looked past him at the stripe of light under Kit's door. As I watched, the light in the room went out and the stripe disappeared. I grabbed Jojo by the sleeve of his sweatshirt. "What did you do to her? Did you hit her? *Did you?*"

He started chuckling. Then, finger by finger, he peeled my hand off his sleeve. Finally he stuck his face near mine and whispered loudly, "Not tonight, little hockey-brother. Least not as I remember. But maybe you'd better ask her in the morning to make sure." He bared all his teeth. "As if it would make any difference to you." Then he turned and walked down the hall toward the staircase.

At the last step before he went up the stairs, Jojo

faced me again. "Oh yeah—too bad you took off after dinner, rough-tough-hockey-boy. You missed the big announcement." He laughed. "It's an announcement you would have liked to hear, since it was about you."

"What was it?" I said. My voice seemed like the only sound in the house.

"Baxter and Mary hauled out the calendar. They finally got it together for this month, see. And guess what? Tomorrow night happens to be your show, brother. Tomorrow night is just for you. Tomorrow night, when your team plays some other team I can't remember, is the official family hockey date for the season, when everyone who wants to can come to see you play. And I think me and Anthony might just feel like taking in a little hockey tomorrow night. Okay with you?"

I shrugged.

"Good," he said. "Sorry about the short notice. But this way," he said, with a nasty wink and more show of teeth, "this way, you won't have too long to get nervous, will you? Good night, rough-tough-hockey-boy. Better practice some of that dukin' on your pillow tonight, huh?"

# fourteen

sually Coach Cooper does not talk about winning or losing. I once heard him tell a parent, "Well, these players don't come out here to *lose* . . ." but the fact is we *do* lose a lot and it must be hard for him to keep everybody pretty happy anyway. Personally, I'm glad he is not one of those coaches who feels he must pretend the team *can* win *every game!!!!* when the players know different. Those coaches are afraid to show even a little "negativity" and so they end up showing zero credibility instead. At the other extreme are coaches who try to fire up their players by talking about how bad the opponents will probably kick our tails, as if this would challenge our pride and inspire us to suddenly grow great talent during warm-ups. The fact is, players know pretty much how good their team is, and how good the other team is, and although they will never play halfhearted against a team they know is superior or cocksure against a team they know is worse, they *do* play with a sense of realism. Coach Cooper is smart enough to leave it to us. He knows we hear everything around the league, he knows we keep the scores in our heads, he knows we are aware of the standings and scoring races and goals against stats. So what more can he tell us?

"You haven't lost five games in a row since the first five games of the season," he says. A lot of us look up, wrinkle our foreheads as we think, then look down between our skates. Is it really that many?

"Think about that," Coach says. He looks around. "Is this the same team that began this season five months ago, losing so bad up in Pennsylvania that they stopped putting the other team's goals up on the board?" The door opens slightly and Shinny slips in, his arm now in a thick cast up to the elbow, white as a new roll of tape.

"I heard that last question, Coach," he says, "and actually, if—"

"Shut up, Shinny. How's the wrist?"

"Fine," says Shinny.

"Good. Now, let's see: Dooby. I ask you, is this

the same team that lost its first five games in a row?"

For once Dooby plays it straight. "No, sir. Same uniforms, different team."

"Anybody want to tell me why? What's different?" He ignores Billy's frantically waving hand. "How about you, Barry?"

Barry hates to talk. He shrugs. "I don't know. Some of the guys, like, got a lot better and stuff, Zip and Woodsie and Ernie and like that. But that's not really why."

"What *is* really why?"

Barry shrugs again. "I don't know. I guess— don't get the wrong idea, Coach—I guess after a couple of games I was kind of ashamed to put on the sweater and go out there. Then it changed, and for a while I didn't care what sweater I had on, there was the chance to play a little hockey. Then—" He looks up and around the room with a fierce frown. "Don't one of you guys give me any grief for this." Then he looks at the coach. "I guess the next stage, like after that music concert most of us played in, was that, all of a sudden, I was actually proud to put on the sweater. I mean, really proud." He looks around again. No one has dared to snicker. "To tell you the truth, I like putting it on this year even better than last year, when we won everything so easy."

The coach nods. He looks at Woodsie, who is also shy. "What do you think, Woodser? You feel different?"

Woodsie speaks evenly. "This team has no excuse for losing five games in a row. A few months ago, we had no excuse for thinking we could do anything *but* that."

"Hmm," says the Coach, "'no excuse.' That's strong stuff to say. Strong stuff, isn't it, Boot?"

It goes quiet and everybody swivels to look at me, but I just say, "It isn't nearly as 'strong' to say as it is to go out and *do* it. Last week we could have talked about how nasty losing *four* in a row might feel. Well—here we are. How does it feel?" Nobody answers. I say, "The Boot believes he can declare that it feels about like needing to puke a bad dinner."

The coach nods. He looks around. Everybody meets his eyes. Finally he says, "Anybody need to puke? No? Well, then, how about this: Anybody need to feel *good?* I mean, feel *really* good?"

Everyone rattles his spears.

"Then let's by all means go out and win. *But*"—he holds up a finger and the few eager guys who were ready to go eat the opponents by the handful hesitate in mid-sprint—"*But.* Let me remind you that feeling good doesn't start once the buzzer has sounded and you look at a scoreboard full of good news. Feeling good starts the second your skates get wet. Remember: The only way you can be happy with the *score* of a game is by being happy with the *playing* of that game." He drops his hand and smiles. "All right. Go get it."

Just before warm-ups are over he motions me to the bench. Looking at me kind of sternly, he says, "You know about Shinny. And I imagine you've been watching what he brought to that line—to your old line. I'm going to play you back in that spot, with Prince and Cody, but I want to make sure you know one thing." He points right into my mesh face shield. "I want you to forget everything Shinny did, forget his desire to pulverize into dust every player in a different-color sweater. For one thing, you see where it got him—back in an even *bigger* cast. But most important, Boot, is this: I want my *Boot* back. I don't want anyone else. I don't care what things you've decided you need to add to or subtract from your game. As far as I'm concerned, there is only one thing your game lacks. Do you know what it is?"

I had an answer, but something told me he just wanted me to shake my head. I did.

He leaned a little closer, and took his finger down. "The only thing your game lacks right now is *you*. You're trying to be someone else. Stop it. Be Boot. Relax and enjoy yourself. And score me three or four goals if you happen to think of it."

"There is never a time," I say, "when the Boot is not thinking of scoring three or four goals."

The buzzer ends warm-ups, the lines set up, the ref drops the puck. Prince ties up the Wharton center's stick and the puck just sits there, so the Boot goes after it. He is cross-checked hard from behind once and then a second time *harder* and his head snaps back as he is knocked to his knees, but he keeps sliding in the right direction and manages to flick the puck over to Cody on the other side, just as he would have done had he *not* been crunched, Cody tears into the zone and draws one defenseman and the winger checking him, leaving only a single D to cover the slot. The Boot scrambles to his skates, leaving his man behind to deliver another cross-check that doesn't land, and then the Boot crosses the blue line and skates hard straight between the circles, right at the defenseman. The Boot taps his stick twice, hard, on the ice to call for the puck and Cody, now mobbed by the two guys closing on him, slings it blind. The Boot races for the puck in the high slot hard and low and he gets to it exactly three-tenths of a second before the defenseman does, and of course they crash right into each other. But the Boot was lower with his shoulders, and besides, he was concentrating on the puck and he *got* it, never mind about that huge weight he has to hump off his back even though it skews his skates sideways and keeps him from snapping the puck in *quite* the spot near the tip of his stick blade that he *prefers* to use for high backhands. He gets a shot off anyway, and the goalie gets his blocker in front of it, but the shot is a toppler—which means the puck just keeps rolling, up his blocker pad and across his bicep and, once it has run out of body, down to the ice and across the line all the way to the back of the net.

By this time the Boot is lying on the ice with his head closest to the right corner of the cage. The back of his neck hurts from the cross-check, and his right knee feels twisted from the collision with the defenseman, and in his stick he does not feel the special magic he likes to feel of a clean puck cleanly seen and cleanly released and cleanly saucered past the goalie into the clean twine. Instead, he feels he has been beat up from the front and the back, has fallen down twice in very awkward fashion, and almost as an afterthought has hacked a cheap backhander end-over-end in the general direction of the cage.

He has scored his first goal while being checked.

Later, Prince tells the Boot that all the way back to the bench the Boot was hollering "I *like* it! I *like* it!" and "There's no turning back now!" over and over, much to the confusion of the opposing players and coaches. It is not true that every shift produces a scramble in the slot, much less a goal; but every shift *does* produce a puck or a place to focus on, and if another player gets in the way he is simply not considered to be a serious obstacle. If he is skating with the puck and the Boot wants it, the Boot concentrates on the puck and as a kind of side effect happens to knock the player down. If the opposing center is set up in the lower circle to the left of Zip, poised to take a pass, and the Boot believes *he* is better qualified to occupy that spot, then the Boot simply moves to occupy it. The center may be sent flying, but that seems a matter of no importance.

Although I cannot deny that this more physically unrestrained style of play seems to have a pretty good effect—*everybody* seems to be crashing around, and halfway through the period I notice the other team's guys are getting rid of the puck earlier and dodging to the side when we skate hard at them and kind of creeping into the zone when they carry the puck instead of blazing—I am not completely comfortable with what's going on. It seems like bodies are flying, but not like anyone is doing any direct, intentional *hitting*. Between shifts I ask Prince about it.

He nods. "Let me ask you something. How many of the goals you have scored in your life have been accidental? I mean, you know, the puck slipped off your stick but a defenseman kicked it and it ricocheted off the shaft of your stick above your glove and dinged the far post and went in. Or you fanned on a big slapper from the high slot and topped the puck so it just trickled off to the side, but the goalie had flopped to stop the slapper and your weeny little roller got by him all ugly and sickly? You score a lot of goals like that?"

"Never," I say. "Every goal the Boot has scored has come straight from a good, clear shot."

Prince nods. "See, that's what you've been allowed to believe. Just like you believe you play this carefully designed strategy thing, sneaking around and stuff, nobody sees you. Well, sorry to tell you, but it's all bogus, Bootsy. How is somebody not going to see you? Of course they see you. You just work hard as a coal miner to get open, that's all, and you do it without noticing the work. I've seen you bust through three guys, elbows up and shoulders straight and bodies flailing, your stick blade on the ice like an immovable piece of pig iron, and you didn't know it because you were just waiting for a pass." He looks at me and I must look shocked because he laughs. "Look, Boot—if you really played according to your hide-and-seek plan, you'd spend the whole game off by yourself, always looking in the wrong direction, wondering when the game was going to begin, with passes and shots and hits and rushes whizzing by you."

"And then someone would come by and knock me flat onto my face," I say.

"Right." We watch as a flashy winger who had obviously done a couple of weeks of stickhandling school last summer bears down on Woodsie, danglin' and twirlin', until he just can't help dropping his eyes for a quick little peek at how slick his blade is, and just then Woodsie jumps in his chest and flattens him, calmly skating away with the puck.

"So you're saying it's really sort of unintentional, all this hitting and stuff."

Prince shakes his head. "Not at all. You go *out* there with all the intention in the world. You intend to get the puck when you want it, get the ice you want, stop the person you want to stop—basically, you just decide you are ready for whatever comes up that needs to be done. That includes hitting whoever comes up that needs to be hit."

He stands up; it's our shift. As we line up for the face-off, I decide to test his theory that it's all just improvised. Out of the corner of my eye I line up the winger opposite me. He's watching for the puck to drop with complete concentration, in hockey position, weight heavy on his skates—it should be easy to jump him before he has a chance to close his mouth. I tense my legs, knot my arms.

The puck drops. I lunge at the winger. He's gone, and I fall heavily onto my right side.

As I am climbing back up, Prince skates slowly by and says, "You're a very naughty Boot, aren't you? Trying to mug that poor gorilla. Just be patient. Some goon will pop up in front of you before long and *then* you'll make him vanish—poof!"

Our line is on the ice when the buzzer sounds to end the first period. Skating back to the bench, I take a look around the stands. Baxter and Mary are standing about six rows up from a blue line, clapping and grinning and waving. They are wearing Wings sweaters. Beside Mary stands Kit in a gray dress, arms crossed tight over her chest, unsmiling, staring at me grimly as if she were looking for signs of a disease. To her left, with one beefy arm thrown over her stiff bony shoulders with obvious show-manship, stands Jojo. He is waving his other arm at me even harder than Baxter, and sneering with all of his teeth. Anthony sits on the end of the row, spider-legs cocked up on the seats in front of him, head turned to watch the Zamboni emerge, with an expression of complete boredom.

As I skate to the bench I suffer another defla-tion of my new tough-guy spirit. Sure, I am play-ing physical hockey today, and sure, my crashing around is even having a sort of inspirational effect on my teammates—we are definitely dominating the game, especially when my unit is on the ice (Cody and Dooby also have goals, and with the two of them I have killed off three penalties without allowing a shot on goal). But it is clear I am not exactly making a grand individual impression as the superbad-deadly-dangerous-jump-back-don't-mess dude I would like to be: Jojo, with his arm on Kit and his sneer, certainly doesn't look especially impressed.

*   *   *

The second period starts. It soon becomes obvious we are tired from all the banging we did, and won't be able to keep it up forever. We restrain ourselves and keep our cool, but our opponents seize this as a chance to jump in *our* faces and take over some room to skate. Woodsie, routinely picking up a dump behind the net, gets clobbered and the guy who hits him snakes in a wraparound; three minutes later their top center simply elbows Cody off the puck at center ice and skates in all alone for a breakaway that cuts our lead to 4-2. We recover some hostility after that, but more from disgust with ourselves than high spirits. Ten seconds from the end of the period, Barry hooks down a left wing from behind, so the third starts on a power play and they score right away on a deflected point shot Zip never sees.

I am skating hard, following Prince's advice, throwing myself all over the place to try to be there whenever a chance to pop someone comes up, but all I get for it is glancing blows against bodies and full impacts against the boards. I get caught out of position several times chasing the puck in our defensive zone, and we are lucky they muff a couple of passes that would have let them capitalize. The momentum has definitely shifted: Now *they* are the ones swirling around, flattening us almost as afterthoughts, swiping the puck time after time, harassing our defensemen every time they go back to get the puck deep in our zone, forechecking, backchecking, putting us on the ice whenever they want. Then the winger I am supposed to check comes wheeling out of the zone with the puck and I am right there with him, and I think, "This is it! This is the chance to turn it around!" So just as he crosses the top of the circle, I drop low and swing a mighty hip at his pants, waiting for the impact that will send him spinning butt-up through the air with a humiliating loss of all bodily control.

The trouble is, just as I swing my hip low he slides the puck past me to the inside and leaps high to the outside, leaving me to spin in two complete 360s while he dekes Zip to his back and flips in the tying goal.

"My fault," I tell Zip as I fish the puck out from behind him. "Sorry, man." He is too mad even to snap at me.

I cannot help glancing up into the stands. Baxter and Mary are sitting with studied neutral expressions on their face, Anthony is clapping slowly, and Jojo, laughing, has both arms around Kit and is trying to kiss her. Baxter looks over and says something sharp to him and he backs off, but only a little. He sees me watching and gives me a thumbs-up sign.

There is just more than a minute left. Now we have to concentrate. Now we can't worry about delivering hits or capitalizing on intimidation. Now it is just hockey: face-offs, passes, poke checks, saves, clears, shots. I think through all of these things like a checklist as I line up for the face-off.

But what did Prince say after all? That checklists are not hockey—that in fact while you are ticking off the items on your neat little list, the madness is happening all around you, and miraculously coming together for a half-second of opportunity that you had better be ready for. That while the Boot watches for his design to emerge, everyone else is hard at whatever work pops up to be done.

Just as I am thinking this, the ref drops the puck. Prince ties up the other center's stick, and I see the center pull his skate back to kick the puck over to the winger across from me. Without thinking, I lunge over to intercept the kick-pass with my own skate and slant the puck just past their defenseman and into the zone. The winger has grabbed my stick to slow me down, but I am running like a desperate crazy man for the puck as the defenseman, with a late jump, tries to cut me off. I jerk hard on my stick and it comes free, and for some reason—the power with which I jerked, the arc of the stick as it slipped out of the winger's grasp—for some reason I slip my other hand onto the shaft and just let the momentum whip me through a wild slap shot from two feet inside the blue line, two feet out from the boards. I would *never* shoot from here. But I get all of this one, a tenth of a second before the diving defenseman knocks my stick out of my hands with his own. But he is too late. As if it is in slow motion, the puck, tracked by my vision, sails on a line toward the inverted-V opening between the goalie's pads, approaching as they close, and I watch in wonder to see whether he will squeeze them shut just before the puck slips through. He does not. The puck hits the back of the net behind him. We lead, 5–4.

My linemates mob me a little but I brush them off. I want to get this thing going again, finish this game with something great. I can feel it coming. This time Prince loses the face-off and they set up a well-formed rush from the defense forward and come right at us, full speed. We are all backskating, their center is almost between the circles looking to deal the puck, the wingers are cutting for the net, it looks suddenly like we are not even a part of the game—but out of nowhere Cody has darted at the puck and picked it off the center's stick and is now burning up the ice all alone.

Now, I know very well no one can catch Cody. Nevertheless, when I see the enemy left wing hop free and take off head-down all-out in Cody's wake, I find myself doing the same. We are all skating as hard as we can push, like three train cars with Cody as the engine. I don't know if Cody even knows he's being tailed; up ahead, past the shoulders of the enemy wing, I see Codes look up at the goalie and drag his skates for a second to start his lateral deke. This is all the hustling winger needs: He swoops his stick in beneath Cody's and taps the puck ahead, wheeling into a big curve in front of his own net, crossing over to pick up speed, and using every bit of momentum from his rink-long dash to turn him back the other way. I steal a glance around, and my spine goes cold when I see that every single Wing has followed Cody and is now facing the wrong way. This kid will have a breakaway with plenty of time to bury it.

But then, just as he is streaking up ice and is about to pass me (facing the wrong way too), it suddenly occurs to me to slide in front of him and just let him use all that speed and grace and force to dash himself against my big old unmoving hulk. So I slide sideways right into his path, and just before I duck my head I see his eyes suddenly take it all in; I can see he's alarmed but most of all he just completely cannot believe that such a dorky obstacle can stop his fabulous rush. Then he hits, and we both fly all over the place and twist and bounce and slam, and when we stop I swear I have taken a couple of his limbs and he has some of mine. I start to laugh, but then I hear a strange sound, and I realize he is whimpering. Crying. Bawling. Then the buzzer sounds and we have won.

* * *

I scramble to my skates in time to see that Woodsie must have picked up the puck after the collision and ragged it for the remaining twenty seconds or so, and I am all set to whoop his name when suddenly a fist hits me square in the forehead and I stagger back against the boards. I notice too late that my helmet has flown off, and that a huge defenseman wants to hit me again in my exposed face.

But I am ready. I must have noticed that he is one of the cool dudes who skates around with the straps that hold his face cage dangling loose, because without thinking I have shaken off my gloves, grabbed the bottom of his cage down near his chin, yanked it up and open, and then driven my right hand as far as I could into his flesh. In fact, I drive my hand in three or four or five times, until I realize the only reason the kid is partially upright is that I am still holding his cage. I drop it. He falls, and starts to whimper just like his buddy.

The ref is skating over to me fast, and I can also feel nausea rising in my throat. But before I get hustled off to the dressing room or puke with shame or both, I remember one last effort I have to make, to take advantage of one of those split-second opportunities. Picking up a stick from the ice, I skate away from the ref and look for my family. They are about twenty feet away, pressed against the glass, everyone but Kit looking with horror at the kid on the ice. They don't even see me coming, so I skeet to a stop right in front of Jojo and, using two hands as if it were an axe, I smash the stick against the glass an inch from his face.

He leaps back and looks at me wildly. I point at him, point at the corner of the rink where the gate is, and take off, three steps ahead of the referee. I skeet to a stop again and jump through the gate and look his way. I am not really surprised he didn't follow my order to meet me. It was mostly for effect anyway.

Fighting the nausea in my throat as my shame threatens to catch up with me and force me to see how ugly I am having to be, I walk by Baxter and Mary and Kit and take the fat part of Jojo's Marilyn Manson sweatshirt in my fist.

"We need to discuss your homework habits," I say.

Anthony, a good six feet past Jojo, laughs softly. "Man be bad *now*," he says. "Man want to talk homework, Jo, you best talk some *homework*."

"Sure," says Jojo. His voice is runny. So is his nose; he sniffs. "Sorry," he apologizes.

"Touch anybody in this family smaller than you and I will deal with it," I say. "Do you understand?"

He tries to nod. Behind me I feel Baxter's hands, soft on my back; I am almost sick but I have to finish.

"Last: If you need help with your homework, you *ask* for it. You say *please*, got it?"

"Right, sure."

I am out of gas, so I jam him down as hard as I can manage and hope he doesn't see that I am losing it, and I turn away and past some part of Baxter or Mary and the referee, and somehow find my way to the locker room. And funny thing—once I have closed the door on all the ugly stuff, once I am in there with my teammates and they are hollering at me and calling me "boulder" and the tape balls are whizzing by and the whole place smells like the worst grungiest thing you ever found in the back of your refrigerator after you got back from a month of summer vacation— well, then, for some reason I don't feel sick anymore. In fact, I don't feel bad at all. I feel pretty good. Pretty good indeed.

Here's a sneak peek at the next book in the

**Wolfbay Wings** ice hockey

series by Bruce Brooks

available from HarperCollins

**7** am panting like a dog running from a rainstorm as I barely make it to the bench and bang through the next line of players going out, and *they* make it all the more bangy because they have to try to clang us on the shoulders and helmets and say nice things and stuff. I finally reach my spot and flop on my pants and hang my head, sucking at the air. It was a long shift. Best shift I ever had, but *long*.

Dooby, however, seems fresh as a new puddle. He drops down next to me and shoves the butt end of his stick, all nasty with black-edged adhesive tape he hasn't changed since our first tie-up against my face mask.

"And—yes, Phil, am I—?" I sneak a look up and see he's holding his other hand to his off-ear the way those color-guys on the Deuce do. "Yes, okay—" He puts on a big fake grin and turns to me. "We're here with the man they call Prince," he says, "and, heh heh, I don't think I'd be stretching it to say he just had himself a *king*-sized shift out there against this highly favored Squirt-A team from Montrose. Now, just for the record, Your Highness—I *may* call you Your Highness, may I not?"

"You better," I pant.

"Right!" He fake-smiles. "Now, as I say, just for the record—*how* many assists *did* you amass during that single shift? The princely number of two, was it not?"

It was three. "Four," I say.

His eyebrows shoot up and he makes as if he's hearing something over his earphone. "My statisticians must have missed one, heh heh. They have you down for three and since that's the number of goals your team actually scored—"

"But I got two on Cody's second, see. Two assists on one goal." You can't get two on one, of course.

"Two on a single goal?" He frowns.

I nod. Before I can start to speak, Woodsie hipchecks Montrose's star center Kenny Moseby and jacks him a foot off the ice, pins him up there long enough for the puck to skitter back to our winger backchecking, then pulls away to let

Moseby fall in a heap. Dooby and I both holler at Woodsie. Moseby doesn't fall in a heap very often.

"Where were we?" Dooby says, shoving his stick back at me.

"I passed it to Cody. He passed it back to me and I shot, but Cheerios got it with a pad and Cody snapped in the 'bound. Now, the rules say the last two men on the scoring team to *pass* the puck—"

"Is it your Canadian heritage that allows you to collect such a gaudy statistic as three assists on one shift, Mr. Prince, sir? You *are* Canadian, yes? Even French-Canadian, if I am not mistaken?

*"Mais oui."*

"Does this give you that little extra edge—ha ha, skates have an edge, see, ha ha—over your relatively latecoming American counterparts *watch the cherry picker!"*

Moseby was hanging out at the red line and his defenseman knew it and flung the puck up the boards behind our D and it should be a breakaway, except Woodsie was playing pretty far back and gets enough of an angle on Moseby that he can mess with Kenny's stick from behind, and Moseby only gets off what is for *him* a half-decent shot. That is to say, a ripping high one, looks like a speeding dime, headed for the very edge inside the far corner but Zip throws up his blocker and Woodsie beats Moseby to his own rebound.

"Not *that* particular American," I say, pointing to Kenny.

"Yes, well, Kenny is what *we* down here call 'special,'" says Dooby. "Speaking of which—how can you read defensemen so well, Mr. Prince? You seem to know how they are going to move, what passing lanes they are going to open up for you, before—ha ha!—they themselves do! Now is *that* perhaps where your hypersensitive rhythmic African-American naturally-improvisatory instincto-athletic voodoo jazz-from-New-Orleans gift comes into play?"

"Yassuh," I say. "It sho' be."

"Thank you." He pulls the stick-end back. On the ice, Moseby almost picks off a sloppy pass to break in alone on Zip, whom he usually eats alive. If K weren't being double-shifted he would have had the legs. But if he weren't being double-shifted, he might not have been out there to try.

"This politically sensitive interview with our international . . ."

I let Dooby fade out. I am in fact tired. It is the third period of an away game against our most hated rivals and we *did* just get three goals on one shift, two by Cody and one by Dooby himself, to stun everybody and take a three-goal lead. The fact that we were tied, with only four minutes left in the game, was shocking enough. Montrose is an awesome hockey machine, put together player by player with keen loving care by their coach, Marco, who stole our best four or five players from last year—including Kenny—as part of his scheme. They have lost only one game, to a team from Philadelphia, in OT. They beat us by one goal the first time we played them, a great showing for us that was the turnaround in our season. Frankly, even though we've only won a handful since then, we knew we'd kick their tails today.

It's my line's turn, out for the last shift of the game. Marco has rested Kenny for a shift but now has him at left wing, where he is playing opposite Boot, our slowest player, but one of our smartest. But even with double the smarts, Boot won't even know where Kenny went to in three seconds.

"Think you'll get three *this* time?" sneers the Montrose center, a kid named Jon who *used* to be a friend of mine until he jumped ship.

"Probably not," I say. I look up at the scoreboard, where it says 6–3, us. "Think *you* will?"

"No prob," he says, and promptly wins the face-off from me. The defenseman dumps, Moseby beats Dooby to the puck between the corner and the cage and—I swear it's intentional, believe me, he's that kind of kid—snaps a blind backhander high off the middle of Zip's back while Zip, facing forward, watches helplessly over his shoulder. Of course the puck topples into the net. 6–4.

"That's one," says the center, as we set again for the face-off. He checks the clock. "Took eight seconds."

"Yeah, but you cheated," I say, as the ref shows the puck.

"How so?"

"You held on to your stick," I say, ignoring the puck as it drops and snapping my stick's heel down hard on the spot where the aluminum shaft of his glitzy model attaches to the wooden blade. The joint pops. They always pop if you hit them right. The guy is left staring at his nice sixty-dollar metal shaft as I kick the puck wide, away from Moseby's side, to Barry out on the left wing. He works it to Cody and I leave the other center deciding whether to get another stick from the bench or haul me down. He grabs my sleeve, but he waited too long. I'm gone. Cody works it in three-on-two perfect until Moseby hustles back to even it out as Codes whips it to was-open-just-a-*second*-ago me, but I drop it between my legs hoping Dooby is trailing. He is. He winds up, fakes a huge slapshot, two defensemen drop to the ice, but Doobs just skates with the puck behind the net and all the way down the boards to the other end, where he stops dead with it behind Zip. Nobody but Marco has figured out yet that Dooby's more interested in killing time than scoring, so it takes them a while to get in and forecheck and by then he has plenty of us to play catch with, and we kill out the clock without letting Moseby touch the puck. At least three times we pass it right by the bladeless center, who can't stop it with his bladeless shaft.

The buzzer ends it. As the rest of the guys

whoop it up—hey, we *hate* these jerks, and it's only their *second* loss—I skate by the kid holding his shaft. It's kind of a light purple, and it has a famous center's signature painted on it.

"You can have a new blade installed on that baby in fifteen minutes," I say. "Good as new. Be calling you 'Mess' next game for sure.

"I been brought up to expect colored people to use cheap tricks," he says. "I should have known."

"I been brought up to expect colored people to use *smart* tricks," I say. "And if you want to talk about something you should have known, then maybe you should have known your own equipment, Caucasian. Never take a big face-off with one of those tin sticks."

"This used to be *our* sport," he says, as I skate off.

I laugh. He doesn't know what he's talking about too many ways to mess with—I wish he could hear Dooby's interview. I want to go rub Zip's facemask and sing a couple of cool songs in the locker room and throw a little balled-up tape at Dooby's big head. And I want to review those three assists—two of them backhand, just past defenders

I held eye-contact with, one of the passes threaded through *two* sets of Montrose legs to Cody at the corner of the net. I needn't worry about that part, though. My French Canadian grandfather, who has never missed even one of my *practices*, will tell me all about them in the car home. In detail. In French. Hey, I love America, I talk the talk here, but I have to tell you—hockey rules, and not only that, it just sounds better in French, *tu sais?*